Caroline Rosina Derby

Salem

A Tale of the Seventeenth Century

Caroline Rosina Derby

Salem
A Tale of the Seventeenth Century

ISBN/EAN: 9783743353657

Manufactured in Europe, USA, Canada, Australia, Japa

Cover: Foto ©Andreas Hilbeck / pixelio.de

Manufactured and distributed by brebook publishing software (www.brebook.com)

Caroline Rosina Derby

Salem

SALEM:

A TALE OF THE SEVENTEENTH CENTURY.

By D. R. CASTLETON.

NEW YORK:

HARPER & BROTHERS, PUBLISHERS,

FRANKLIN SQUARE.

1874.

PREFACE.

THE requirements of literary conventionality seem to demand a preface as a necessary adjunct of a book—we had nearly written a necessary *evil;* and as the beaten path is acknowledged to be the safest, we yield in cheerful acquiescence—although to call that a *preface* which is usually written after the book is completed, would seem to unassisted reason very like a misnomer.

In giving the accompanying pages to the public, we would only say that it has seemed well to us that the widespread and terrible delusion, which so nearly made shipwreck of our infant colony at the close of the seventeenth century, should not be suffered to sink into oblivion. We know, indeed, that the more practiced hand of an able and faithful historian has already put it upon record in a masterly way, and in so doing has made a rich and valuable contribution to our national literature. But these books, though deeply interesting, are too valuable and too weighty to be found in free circulation among general readers; and we have been surprised to find how very vague and incorrect was the knowledge of this subject in many cultivated persons who were well-informed on other matters of history.

We have endeavored with careful hand to retouch the rapidly fading picture—to call up again to view the scenes and actors of those terrible times; and if in so doing we have ventured " to twine round history's legends dim the glowing roses of romance," it was only to heighten the effect of the picture, and to enable us to give a clearer idea of the persons who composed the little community as it then existed—their habits, and modes of life and thought.

In all that is purely historical we claim to be strictly authentic: such portions being either copies from the court records, or carefully compiled from the most reliable historians. Our own feet have trodden the precincts of "Salem Village," of "Gallow's Hill," and "Prison Lane;" in our own hands we have held the veritable "witch-pins;" our own eyes have searched the records, and read one of the original death-warrants still in preservation—and therefore we claim to know something of that of which we have written.

It is a matter of regret to us that in a tale so peculiarly New England in its character we could not venture to introduce "the live Yankee."

The quaint phraseology is easily hit off, and the strange mixture of shrewd intelligence and original comicality would have served to give a perhaps needed sparkle to our pages; but historical exigences, to which we felt bound to adhere, forbade the tempting anachronism.

The Yankee is an amalgam which had not then issued from the crucible of the ages; the strange ubiquitous creature, ever upon his feet, ever ready with hand and speech, had not then asserted himself; and we had no warrant for chipping the egg-shell of Time, in which he was then fussily inchoating.

In conclusion, we will say, in the borrowed words of an apocryphal writer, "If I have done well, and as is fitting the story, it is that which I desired; but if slenderly and meanly, it is that which I could attain unto."

CHAPTER I.

HOMESICKNESS.

"Hame!—hame!—hame!
  Oh! it's hame, hame, I fain wad be;
Hame—hame—hame—
  In my ain countrie!"

IT was midwinter in New England, the very commencement of the year 1679—a year made ever memorable to the little colony settled along the shores of the Massachusetts Bay, as one of the coldest, hardest, and most disastrous which the new dwellers on that rugged and inhospitable coast had yet encountered. Storm and shipwreck had walked in devastation upon the angry and tumultuous waters, and cold, famine, and sickness had desolated the land, and threatened to depopulate its shores. Many of the older settlers trembled for the success of their costly experiment, fearing the land was too sterile and inhospitable ever to give them a permanent home; and many among the more newly arrived would gladly have returned to the shores they had reluctantly parted from, had not the wild and stormy main rolled as an impassable barrier between them and the sadly lamented homes they had deserted.

It was in the height of one of those long, fierce, pitiless northeastern storms of mingled rain, snow, sleet, cold, and tempest, which even now smite with such bitter force upon our bleak New England shores, sweeping the shrieking seamen down to their unknown graves, wrecking the hopes of our "merchant princes," and making even the listening landsmen shudder in their sheltered homes — clouds and darkness brooded over the face of the seething deep, whose fierce billows broke on the wide-resounding shore with a reverberation like thunder. The day had been cheerless enough, unvisited by a single gleam of sunshine, and now, as night began to close in over the sodden landscape, the tempest seemed to gather more force, and grow hour by hour more dreary and awful.

In a chamber of a small house, in the then

newly settled town of Salem, two persons, a woman and a little child, sat alone, and listened in awe to the fierce blasts of wind, which, rushing in from the angry sea, rocked their dwelling to its very foundations.

They were new-comers, and had been passengers in the latest vessel which came over in the preceding autumn. They were evidently Scottish by birth—the woman, who might have been about fifty-five years of age, was still an erect and handsome woman, though something of the sternness of purpose which marked the old Scotch Covenanters might possibly have been traced in her regular but strongly marked features. She held upon her lap a struggling child of six or seven years of age—a beautiful girl, in whose fair face, though now distorted by passionate weeping, might be read much of the beauty as well as the strong self-will which marked the face of the grand-mother.

"Whist, Allie; whist, my bonnie bairn! weel ye?—dinna ye greet sae sair," said the woman tenderly, folding the sobbing child to her bosom. "Hush! hush! my ain precious pet; dinna ye sab an' greet sae, my ain Allie's wee Allie—whist, noo, whist!"

"Hame! hame!—I will gae hame!" sobbed the child passionately. "I *maun* gae hame; I *will* gae hame; I winna bide here. Let me gang hame, grannie."

"Whist! whist! noo, Allie, my ain son-sie bairn, ye are na' wiselike tae talk in that fashion, for weel ye ken ye kinna gae hame."

"But I *will*—I *will!*" shouted the imperi-ous child. "I will gae hame—I *will*, I *will*; an' wha' shall stay me? Let me gang, gran-nie."

"Stop, stop! my ain little lass; my bon-nie wee birdie! stop, an' hear 'till me; ye *are* at hame—*this* is yer hame, Allie; ye ha' nae ither; quit greetin' noo, my sonsie bairn, an' listen tae me."

"I winna listen—nor I winna stop greet-in' till ye tak' me hame; *hame!* grannie, tak' me *hame!*"

"Silly bairnie; an' do ye na' ken this is yer hame?"

"Na', na'—it's *na'* my hame; I *winna* bide here; I will gae hame to my ain bonny

Scotland; this is nae hame—it is jist an awfu' gruesom' kintra!   I hate it—I *hate* it! I winna bide here—it maks me sair sick; look there, an' see if it is na' awfu'?" and as she spoke she put her little, strong arm round her grandmother's neck, and forcibly turned her head to the window to which she pointed.

The view from the window, thus indicated by the impatient little hand, was certainly lugubrious enough to warrant the child's distaste. The house in which the two speakers were sitting was the very last one in the row which then constituted the straggling, narrow, crooked little Main (now Essex) Street of the small, irregular, and unpretending little town of Salem, and stood, consequently, nearest to the water; and the view from the window to which the childish hand so impetuously pointed consisted of a plain of discolored but untrodden snow, stretching from the house down to the very shore, where, piled up in wild and chaotic confusion, were huge black rocks, coated on one side with gathered snow and sleet, and mingled with them massive cakes of shattered and jagged ice, which, broken up by the combined force of wind and waves, had been driven in and heaped up in ghastly desolation upon the shore. Beyond these was a dull margin of ice, and, still beyond, sullen and fierce rolled the black waters, occasionally iridescent, with a pale, blue, phosphoric light, and then settling down again in inky blackness.

On either hand the prospect was bounded by the dark masses of the forest fir-trees, which crept down almost to the very water's edge, and over all hung like a sable covering the dull, gray, leaden clouds, rayless and gloomy—only changing when some fiercer burst of wind tore them asunder, and tossed them into wilder forms of gloom and portent.

"Luik! luik!" exclaimed the shivering child, turning away in nervous terror as she spoke. "It's gruesom'—it's awfu'! I said sae; it's a wicked lan', an' a hatefu'; I winna bide here."

"Whist! Allie, darlin'! harken ye to me, my bonnie queen, my ain precious wee birdie!" said the woman, soothingly; and as she spoke she rose, and, going to the window, drew the curtain to shut out the sight of the night and the tempest. "Harken to me, my dawtit dearie; wha' do ye ken o' the lan'? ye hae jist kim, ye ken nocht aboot it; it ha' been a' winter yet; wait till ye see the simmer."

"There is nae simmer here," said the child; "there canna be — the simmer wad na' kim here; there are nae bonnie birdies here to sit an' sing in the trees, as they do at hame, an' nae pretty rowanberries for them to eat, gin they wa'; an' the trees — they are na' like our ain trees — they hae nae leaves, they are black, an' stiff, an' awfu'; I hate to luik at them; an' aye whiles they groan an' skreigh like they were in pain. Oh, grannie! dear grannie! tak' me hame to my ain dear Scotland. I *maun*, I *will* gae back to the bonnie Hillside Farm!"

"An' wha' wad ye do, gin ye wa' there, Allie? It wad be winter there too; dinna ye mind that, my sonsie lassie? hae ye forgot that there is winter there too?"

"Na'! na'! not winter like this ane — it wa' niver sic a winter thar as this ane; it wad na' be too cauld to sit on th' auld kirk steps, an' sing wi' th' lave o' them—I hae nae maties here, ye ken. I want auld Sawnie to lap me up in his plaidie, an' pit me on his shoulder, an' awa' to the sheep walks wi' me; an' tak' me to the tap o' Ben Rimmon, an' let me gather the bonnie purple heather. I want auld Tibbie to tak' me by the han', an' I gae wi' her to the byre, an' see her milk the coos, an' pick up the dook's eggs, an' see wha' the auld big goosie is sitting ahint the mow—oh! I *maun* gae, I *will* gae."

"Harken ye to this, my dawtit lass: Sawnie an' auld Tib are na' at the Hillside Farm the noo; they hae gaen awa'—ye wad na' fin' them there noo."

"An' wha' for nae? whar shuld they be gaen?"

"Dinna ye mind Sawnie ha' gaen tae be shepherd to Scott o' the Burnside; an' Tibbie ha' gaen to keep housie for her brither? They wad be baith awa'."

"Weel-a-weel!" said Alice, a little startled at this intelligence; "but they wad baith win bock agin, grandmither, gin *we* were there—they wad."

"Na', na', Alice," said the grandmother,

sadly, for the child's persistence had roused her own regrets; "they wad na' kim bock agin—we sall see them nae mair."

"Weel, we could gae to the Hillside Farm, ony way; I want to rin doon the bra', an' crass the brig abune the little burn, an' pu' the gowans—I *kin* do tha'."

"Na', na', Alice, my bonnie bairn. Ye forget I hae sold the Hillside Farm; ye canna gae bock there—it is our hame nae mair."

"Buy it bock agin, grannie—buy it bock agin; I *maun*, I *will* gae bock."

"Na', my Alice! I canna buy it bock; it wa' for yer sak', dearie, that I left it, an' crossed the wide stormy waters, to fin' a safe hame for ye; an' noo ye *maun* bide here!"

"Oh! I winna; I winna—I will gae hame!"

"Haith! Alice; dinna say that agin; ye are as fou' as a goshawk; ye mind nocht I say till ye; I thought ye were mair sinsible an' wiselike. Heck, sirs! an' kinna ye mind hoo sick ye wa' in the big ship, an' we comin' here; an' hoo ye used to greet, and skirl out that the ship wa' gaen *doon—doon*—an' ye wad sure be droon'd; an' ye fritting an' fritting a' the way? an' wad ye like to thry it agin, think ye?"

"'Deed, thin, an' I *wad;* thry me, grannie! thry me; on'y tak' ship an' thry me; I winna greet—I winna frit—I will be patient—I will be good; on'y tak' me hame. to my ain bonnie Scotland."

"But, Alice, think ye; there is niver a way ye kin gang; dinna ye ken the last ship ha' sailed? there'll be nae mair until the spring."

"Then throw me into the water, grannie, and let my bodie float hame to Scotland."

"Whist! Allie; my sonsie dochter! I aye thought ye wa' mair cannie an' douce; ye are jist fou', Allie; dinna ye think the fish wad ate you; dinna ye mind hoo yer wad cry out in yer sleep, and say ye harkit the big fishes rubbin' their heads agin the ship's sides, an' wad pray me na' to let them bite ye?"

"Yes! yes! I mind it a'; but I wad na' care noo; they might swallow me if they wad, like as they did the auld prophet mon, if aiblins they wad bring me to my ain dear land, and pit me out there. Oh! I'm sair sick at heart, an' I'll dee here, grandmither, gin ye dinna tak' me hame."

"Oh! wae is me! wae is me!" cried the wearied and discouraged woman, whose own heart was homesick in longings for her native land, to which she was bound by many ties far stronger than any little Alice knew. "Wae's me, wae's me! what iver will I do? I hae nabodie in aw' the wide world but this ane; my ain bonnie dochter, that luved me true, is in her cauld grave, an' the mools abune her head; an' her little wee Allie, my ain bonnie wee Allie, that I hae carried in my bosom sin' the day her puir mither deed —she dinna care for me noo. Oh! wae's the day!—I hae nathing left to luve."

"Yes, yes; I *do* care for ye, grannie! an' I *do* luve ye," said the child, turning impatiently away from her as she spoke. "But I want to gae hame—I *maun* gae hame—I *will* gae hame!"

"Gae, then," said the grandmother, her own impatient spirit fairly overtasked by the obstinate persistency of the child. "Gae yer ways then—I hae dune wi' ye." And, as she spoke, she removed the child from her knees, and, setting her down upon her feet in the middle of the floor, she turned away from her. "Gae ye, then—do as ye choose; gae where ye loike, an' leave me my lane; I kin but dee; mak' yer way hame to Scotland, if ye will—and whin they ask for the auld grandmither that fed ye an' bred ye, ye kin tell them ye lef' her her lane to dee. Tell them her on'y *ain* child, her bonnie Alice, wa' dead; an' her on'y gran'child, her Alice's wee Allie, rinned awa' fra' her. Oh, haith! dinna ye greet for me—somebodie will lay me in the grave, an' in heaven abune I'll maybe happen fin' my ain true Alice; guid-bye to ye—*ye kin gae.*"

Had the old woman calculated nicely the effect of her words (which she certainly did not, for she was scarcely less impulsive and passionate than the child herself), she could not have chosen any more effectual for her purpose. The stubborn and self-willed spirit, that could not be subdued by opposition, or reached by reason or argument, was conquered by affection, and yielded to a quick burst of repentant love and feeling.

"Oh! I winna gae an' leave ye; I *win-*

na!—I *winna!*—I *do luve* ye—I *do care* for ye—an' I will stay wi' ye, grannie!" she sobbed out in broken words, striving to regain her place upon her grandmother's lap.

But the woman saw her advantage, and with true Scottish shrewdness she hastened to improve it. "Na'! na'!" she said, coldly—putting aside the little clinging arms that tried to clasp her neck, although she felt her whole soul melting in tenderness within her—"na', na'! dinna heed me; dinna tak' tent o' me; gae ye yer ain gate, an' leave me to mine—I'll do weel enou'; gae yer ways—an' fareweel."

"Na', na'! dinna say 'fareweel;' see, I am na' gangin'; I *winna gae;* I am yer ain wee lassie—tak' me in yer lap agin—kiss me an' luve me, as ye used to do; an' ca' me yer ain dear Alice's wee Allie, an' I will be bidable, an' do jist wha' ye tell me—I *will*, I *will.* There, noo, there!" she said, as she effected her lodgment within the fondly welcoming arms that tenderly embraced her, and hid her little tear-stained cheek upon the faithful bosom that had pillowed her infancy. "Noo say, 'God bless my darlin'!' an' kiss me, an' sing me to sleep, an' I'll luve ye *foriver*, an' *niver* leave ye."

Gladly did the loving arms close round the little repentant one, and long after the little quivering bosom had ceased to sob and sigh, the grandmother sat rocking her to and fro, sadly listening to the voices of the stormy night, and crooning over a low, sweet lullaby — the burden of which was still, "Oh! my ain precious ane! my ain bairn's bairnie! my darlin'; my ain Alice's wee Allie!"

Long into the night she sat thus; and sadder longing for her forsaken home than little Allie ever knew came thronging thick about her; alone in a strange, wild land— the little creature, sobbing in its sleep upon her breast, her only tie to earth. But she was a woman of resolute spirit—she would not look back repiningly; and she set her face as a flint to meet and bear the destiny which her own action had drawn upon her-self.

CHAPTER II.

CHILDHOOD.

> "With hand and fancy active ever—
> Devising, doing, striving still;
> Defeated oft—despairing never,
> Upspringing strong in hope and will."

BUT time rolled on in its resistless course; the night, the storm, and the winter had passed gradually away; and little Alice, whose impressible temperament was like an air-harp, which lends a responsive vibration to every varying breeze that may sweep across it—now swelling out gayly and cheerily as a marriage-bell, now sinking to the minor chords of wailing and sadness—had passed from gloom to gladness. As in the storm and darkness she had been nervously depressed and miserable, so in due proportion did her elastic and buoyant young spirit rise to the full enjoyment of brighter days

and milder airs; perhaps all the more joy-
ously for the very gloom which had preceded them.

The spring, with its abundant promise of
buds and blossoms, its halcyon skies and
fragrant breezes, seemed mirrored in her
clear, sweet blue eyes; and summer itself—
the glorious summer of our New England
climate—with its compensating beauty, its
myriad-hued blossoms, its gayly-plumaged
and sweet-songed birds, drove her nearly
wild with excitement and admiration. She
fairly *reveled* in the universal beauty all
around her: the clear, pure air; the fresh,
tremulous beauty of the tender morning
light, that flushed the eastern skies at new-
born day; the glorious sunsets, which barred
the west with floods of crimson and gold,
had for her ardent and poetic nature an ex-
hilaration she had never known before.

There was now no longer any talk of returning to Scotland; the heather and the
gowans of her native hills, once so fondly
remembered, had shrunk in comparison with
the wide-flung blossoms of our woods and
wilds; her heart was weaned from her early

home—even the beloved "Hillside Farm" was forgotten; she dropped the Scottish dialect which her grandmother still retained, and the little Highland lassie was fast changing into a fair New England maiden. She lived a simple, happy, healthful, wood-land life; out upon the hills or by the ocean's shore, or deep in the dim forest glades, making free acquaintance with benefi-cent nature, and gaining health and strength and beauty from the invigorating breezes.

One day she fairly startled her grand-mother as she darted in at the open door, like some bright-winged tropical bird; her long, fair hair twined with the pale purple flowers of the wild aster, and her neck and arms encircled with chains of bright crimson berries, whose coral hue set off their dazzling whiteness.

"Luke at me!—luke at me, grannie! am I not bonnie?" she said, as she danced in her childish glee and pretty vanity before the eyes of her grandmother. "Am I not your sonsie Allie now? say, luke at me!"

"Oh, my bairn! my bairn!" cried the grandmother, shuddering as she looked at her. "Pu' them aff—pu' them aff! the pawky flowers. I dinna loike to see ye sae, my child! Oh! pu' them aff—pu' them aff, I say."

"No, no!" said little Alice, decidedly; "I loike them—they are pretty. Why dinna ye loike them?"

"Oh!" sighed the poor woman, "ye luke sae loike yer puir mither, it breaks my heart; oh! do go an' tak' them aff." And she turned sadly away.

"Luke loike my mither! and why not? why would'nt I luke loike her? Tell me," she said, persistently following her grandmother with glances of mingled curiosity and anger. "Why do you talk that way for? Ye call my mither yer dear Alice—yer ain dear child; I thought ye luved my mither—I thought you wanted me to be loike her."

"An' so she wa'—an' sae I did—an' sae I do," cried the grandmother, catching the child in her arms in a passionate embrace. "But ye kin na' onderstan', Allie darling! ye are too young; but ye do ken this—ye ken yer mither is deed, an' when ye kim in, lukin' sae loike her, ye took me too sudden, an' gave me a turn loike—as if it wa' her varry sel'. Ah! ye dinna ken, an' lang may it be before ye do, wha' the heart's sorrow is for them it ha' luved an' lost; an' now, my bairnie, rin awa' an' play, an' dinna think I meant to speak cross to ye, my on'y treasure."

And little Alice went back to her birds and her flowers without another word, but with a vague impression upon her mind that there was something about the memory of her mother that she was not permitted to know and must not question. But youth is sanguine, and the cloud, if unforgotten, did not cast a heavy shadow. And so Alice grew up among all the kindly influences of nature; her young life as pure and sweet, and nearly as uncultivated, as the wild flowers she loved.

Of education, in its popular sense (as understood to mean book learning), she had very little, and of accomplishments she knew nothing. Her grandmother was a fairly educated woman, for the times she lived in; she could read and write and keep her simple accounts, and that was all that was then judged important for a woman to know; and this limited amount of knowledge she had taught to her grandchild, who was a quick and retentive pupil; and though she went to school occasionally when opportunity offered, there was little to be gained there, and possibly neither Alice nor her grandmother dreamed there was more for them to know.

The girl was contented—she had no ambitious imaginings, she knew no lot more favored than her own; she had few acquaintances—her position did not admit of it—but she had one friend, her constant companion and welcome attendant in all her wanderings: this was Pashemet, a young Indian lad some years older than herself.

Pashemet belonged to the tribe of the Naumkeags, once a powerful and prosperous race, whose hunting-grounds had included the site of the present town. He was the son of one of the Sagamores, or chiefs, who had embraced Christianity, and had always maintained friendly relations with the white settlers. No two beings could have been imagined less alike than the calm, grave, self-contained Indian lad, and the quick, impulsive, demonstrative daughter of the white race; and yet, in spite of this contrast (or, possibly, in consequence of it), a warm and tender friendship had sprung up between them, and drew them strongly together.

Pashemet was six or seven years older than Alice, and while she looked up to him in loving confidence and warm admiration, he watched over her steps with the tender affection of an elder brother and the careful guardianship of a loving father.

He taught to his delighted listener much of the fanciful lore of his own people; his memory was rich in legends of the rocks and the hills; every brook had its story, every forest its memories; and in return Alice imparted to him the limited education she had received from her grandmother. He taught her to use the Indian bow with an almost unerring aim, to feather the arrows, to weave the nets, to climb the hills, to walk on snow-shoes. He procured her a light Indian canoe, and taught her to guide it over the water with a skill and dexterity scarcely less than his own. He led her to the haunts of the fairest flowers and the earliest fruits.

Seated side by side on some breezy hill, or rocking on the calm blue waters, he told her long legends of the past history of his once widespread but now rapidly diminishing people. He rowed with her over to Castle Hill, and told her of his grandfather Nanepashemet, whose fort was on that hill, and who was killed there, on his own rocky eminence, by the cowardly and treacherous Tarrentines. And when the boy's savage and but half-restrained nature kindled at the remembrance, and the wild desire for vengeance seemed breathing in his swelling veins and trembling on his eager lips, Alice would lay her little, gentle white hand softly upon his tawny one, and tell him of the love of the great "Good Father," and of the happy hunting-grounds reserved for the meek and forgiving; or, seated side by side in some quiet spot, she would teach him to read it for himself.

"Listen! daughter of the pale faces," he said to her one day, as they stood together upon the pebbly margin of a clear, blue pond, whose quiet waters were starred all over with the pure and fragrant blossoms of the white water-lily—" Listen ! Pashemet has no sister, and his mother has gone long ago to the Spirit Land. Pashemet is alone in his wigwam—he has no mother, no sister."

"And I, too," said Alice, answering him in his own strain—" I, too, am the last of my people. I have no father, no brother—I, too, am alone. But see," she said kindly, " I will be your sister, and I will choose you for my brother." Stooping to the cool water which rippled at her feet, she dipped her hand in it, and laid it on the dusky brow of the youth beside her. " Oh, Pashemet ! my brother, I baptize you ' the Fir-tree.' "

Calm, grave, and unsmiling, the Indian boy imitated her graceful action, and as he sprinkled the bright drops over her long, flowing, chestnut curls, he murmured gravely—" Oh, Alice ! my sister, pure and beautiful ! I baptize thee ' the Water-lily.' "

Laughingly Alice's flower-like head bent beneath the mimic shower, but from that moment, as if by tacit consent, they always recognized the assumed bond, and addressed each other by these endearing or fanciful names.

But we are lingering too long over these trivial incidents of our heroine's childhood, and we must ask the indulgence of our readers to skip over a period of a dozen years. A period, indeed, of much importance in the advancement of the little colony, which had, of course, gained much in numbers in that time, partly by natural increase, and still more by new and important arrivals. Much had, of course, been accomplished in a dozen years to improve the little settlement; the town was better organized and better governed; new streets had been laid out; new buildings, and of a better class, had been erected; new sources of industry opened; and a new impetus given to education, commerce, and agriculture.

But—as for the *dramatis personœ* of our story—Mrs. Campbell (Alice's grandmother) was little changed; she was still a hale, handsome, and resolute, though now an elderly woman. But she did not show her years, if she felt them; she had reached that stand-point in life where nature seems to pause and rest herself awhile; the growth and progress of her Spring had long passed by, but the withering desolation of her Winter had not yet begun: for her, it was perhaps the mellow Indian summer of life, serene and beautiful; the busy labors of life gone by, its burden not yet assumed.

But Alice had changed far more; hers was still the season of growth and development. The rich promise of her childhood was more than fulfilled; the Water-lily had bloomed out in all its pure, perfected beauty. She was gloriously fair, but with cheeks and lips vermeil with the fresh hues of health. A figure full and free as Hebe, yet with the light grace of the wild gazelle; with long, dancing, chestnut curls, just touched with gold when the light wind tossed them into the sun's golden rays; and clear blue eyes, in which youth, health, and summer held innocent merriment. As gay and guileless as a child, yet as gentle and loving as a woman—she was the idol of her grandmother, with whom she still lived in the humble home in which we first found her.

But Pashemet, her adopted brother, had gone; his people had removed farther to the West, and the young warrior, who was one day to succeed his father as Sagamore, had of course gone with them. And though Alice remembered him with tender interest, and had once or twice received kindly messages or simple tokens of remembrance from him, brought to her by some wandering Indian of his tribe, who had come back, perhaps, only to look upon the graves of his people, she had not seen him for more than six years.

CHAPTER III.

"'Twas that loveliness, ever in motion, which plays
Like the light upon autumn's soft shadowy days;
Now here and now there, giving warmth as it flies
From the lips to the cheek, from the cheek to the eyes;
And where it most sparkled no glance could discover—
In lip, cheek, or eyes—for she brightened all over."

THE exquisite beauty of one of the long Spring twilights of New England was slowly fading; the glowing west was still a sea of dazzling light and brilliancy; but the amber and gold which had flushed the pure blue of the western sky was gradually turning to purple and crimson, and streaming up in long penciled rays to the zenith, when Goodwife Campbell sat at the front window of her quiet home, silent, and thoughtfully knitting.

But though her active and experienced hands were thus busy, her mind and eyes were not given to the monotonous work which, still turning and lengthening, grew under her restless fingers; mind and eyes were not requisite to the familiar and mechanical task, else would the stocking she was skillfully fashioning have been an utter failure; for her whole attention was given to the view up the street which her window commanded.

The little room in which she sat, although in every way comfortable, according to the very limited requirement of the times, was very simple in its appointments, and would have looked meagre even to bareness to modern eyes; but it was neatness itself, and surely that is in itself a beauty. The bare, whitewashed walls were spotless in their purity; no carpet covered the unpainted floor, but it had been scrubbed white as snow, had been carefully sanded, and the sand freshly " streaked," or brushed into wavy lines and curves of beauty.

The graceful streaking of a sanded floor in this fashion was an accomplishment upon which thrifty housewives greatly prided themselves in those days, and taught its mysteries as an important branch of woman-ly education to their young daughters. The practice was marked by certain rules, the sand being at first dropped about the newly washed floor in small conical heaps of uniform size and at regular distances—this was expected to last for a certain number of days ; then, when busy, passing feet had trampled and scattered it, it was to be carefully streaked, or swept in wavy parallel lines; and when these had in their turn been obliterated, a third fashion of brushing it across in checker-work was admissible: this was expected to close the weekly wear, and bring it round to scrubbing-day again.

The white half-curtains which shaded the spotlessly clean but coarse, knobby glass windows, hung white, fresh, and untumbled in their crisp starchiness; but, besides its crowning grace of neatness, the little room was beautified by slight but decided marks of delicate womanly taste and refinement. Round the tall, narrow looking-glass, on the surface edge of which an ornamental border had been cut in the manufacture of the glass itself, a skillful hand had fastened a thick wreath of shining, dark-green leaves, which, wholly concealing the quaint black frame, made the little mirror look like a cool, quiet lake, smiling out amid the green woods.

On the many-twisted-legged little table under the glass stood a large flat dish of water, its whole surface covered with the sweet pink buds and graceful leaves of the May-flower — first herald of the spring — sending out the perfume of its breath to fill the room; and over the wide mantel-piece stood small, high glasses of dark-green leaves and scarlet berries, arranged with the artistic taste which speaks a loving hand; while in a rude, clumsy-made cage in the side window hung a tame robin, piping his farewell to the day, and coquettishly picking at the fresh chickweed that ornamented his cage. But the little presiding deity of the place—she whose innocent taste had so impressed itself upon these minor arrangements — was not present; and it was in search of her that the grandmother's loving eyes were so often turned to the window.

"Haint she kim yet? Wall! I 'clare I niver see notting to beat dat are!" said old Winny, the colored woman, who was the only help employed in this primitive little household. Two or three times already had she been in on the errand of inquiry, and returned without satisfaction. "I 'clare to yer now, I tink she orter be in ; I dunno'! but I tink it haint nowuz safe for her to' be out, its got so late, and sich a young ting as she is."

"Ye may gang doon to the gate, Winny, an' glint up the street ava', an' see if she's na' kimmin' doon the toun."

Winny obeyed ; she went to the gate, shaded her eyes from the dazzling western brightness, stood at least five minutes gazing persistently up the straggling and irregular street, and then returning, she announced gravely, "She's not comin'. I didn't see a bit of her—not one bit !"

"Weel, weel !" said her mistress, smiling; "I'm gey glad o' that, Winny ; I wad na' wish my bairnie to kim hame in bits, ony way."

The astute Winny meditated for a minute or two in silence over this seemingly strange answer, and then a loud cachinnation told that the point of her mistress's wit had reached her comprehension. "But would it not be more respectabler like, if I was to run up the street and meet her, and fotch her home—say?"

" "Na', na'!" said the grandmother, smiling; "I dinna think ye ha' need to do that. She'll win hame her lane afore the neet fa's, I'm thinkin'."

"Well, if yer say so, I s'pose she will. Of course yer knows best;" and Winny returned to the kitchen.

Another quarter of an hour "dragged its slow length along," and just as the grandmother, beginning to grow really anxious, had risen to lay aside her knitting, in order, probably, to give herself up more fully to the indulgence of her nameless fears, the tramp of a horse's feet at the gate, and a low, sweet burst of ringing, girlish laughter, dispelled them altogether, and she reached the door just in time to see her darling carefully lifted from the pillion by an honest-looking young man, who, with a gay "Good-night to you," rode laughingly away.

"Weel-a-weel! Allie," she said, meeting her at the door; "ye hae bin lang awa', dearie. An' wha's keepin' ye sae late, my bonnie lassie?"

"Oh, I have been a good ways, grandmother, dear. Just let me get my things off, and I'll tell you all."

"But where awa' hae ye bin, lassie? Tell me?"

"I have been up to Nurse's Farm, grannie."

"Nurse's Farm? Wha'! na' up to the village, lassie? Sure, ye dinna mean that?"

"I do, then; I mean just that, grannie."

"My certies! An' wha' for did ye na' tell me, Allie? I hae been sair fashed aboot ye. An' why wa' na' ye tellin' me gin ye wa' goin' there?"

"I did not know it myself, grandmother; but I sent you word though. Did not little Mary English come in and tell you where I was?"

"Niver a whit. I hae na' seen Mary English the day."

"The careless little gipsy! And she promised me so fair, too! Well, never mind; I am sorry if you fretted, though;" and, as she spoke, the girl threw her soft arms round the old woman's neck, and pressed her sweet, rosy lips to the withered cheek. "I am not worth half the trouble you take about me, grandmother; but you see I am all safe, and I have had such a pleasant time."

"Weel-a-weel! an' ye maun tell me a' aboot it, my lassie."

"Yes, indeed, I will; but, grannie, have you not had your supper yet?"

"Nae 'deed; I wa' waitin' for ye. Ye hae na' had yours, hae you?"

"Yes, indeed; I had mine—oh, two hours ago. I'm so sorry you waited. Sit down now and take yours, and I'll sit here, close by you, and tell you all I've heard and seen. You see, I meant to go up only as far as 'Salem Corner;' but it was so pleasant, I kept on just for a walk; when who should come up behind me but Rebecca Preston and Mary Tarbell, Landlord Nurse's two married daughters, and with them their youngest sister, Sarah Nurse. Well, I knew them all, and Sarah Nurse I used to go to school with; and so we walked along talking together, and when I would have turned back they would not hear of it : I must go home with them, and stay to supper, and see their mother. And when I said I could not walk back in the evening, Mary Tarbell said her husband was coming over, and would bring me on a pillion. You know, grannie, I don't get a ride very often, and I did want to go with them; but I said, 'No; I couldn't leave you alone. Not knowing where I was, you might be anxious.' And just then John English came down the road, with his little Mary on behind him; and they stopped them, and Mary said she was coming straight home, and she would run over and tell you where I was, and so I felt easy about that; but I shall give her a bit of a scolding for forgetting it. And, grandmother, it was lovely over there, and they were all so pleasant!"

"An' how wa' Goody Nurse?" inquired the listener.

"Well, she *said* she was pretty bad with the rheumatism, but she was as bright and cheery as a bird. She asked how you was, and if you had your rheumatism now; and I told her you did last winter, but you was a great deal better now. 'I'm glad to hear it,' says she; 'but your grandmother is only a child to me. Why, I'm threescore and ten, and five over,' says she. Only think, grannie; did you think she was as much as that?"

"An' did ye bide till the supper, Allie?"

"Yes, indeed, and there was a tableful. There was Landlord Nurse and Goody, and two of their sons; and there was Thomas Preston and Rebecca, and Mary and John Tarbell, and Elizabeth Russel and her husband, and Sarah Nurse and her bachelor from Marblehead, and I. Only think, what a family—thirteen of us to sit down to supper!"

"Thirteen! Oh, my bairnie! tha's an uncanny number — I dread tha's an unlucky thing. We wad say at hame one of the number wad be deed afore anither year. I dinna like the thirteen."

"Oh! well, grannie, I guess I did not count them right; and, besides, there were ever so many of the little grandchildren running in and out all the time. I guess that won't hurt us; and we were as gay as larks."

"An' tell me, wha' had ye for the supper, lassie? It maun tak' a deal to feed sae mony."

"My goodness! you'd think so. There was every thing: fried bacon and eggs, and cold boiled beef, and baked beans, and minced salt fish, and roasted potatoes, and pickles, and hot Indian bread, and white bread, and cake, and pies, and preserved barberries, and honey, and milk, and cider. Oh! and, by the way, that makes me think—Goody Nurse asked me how your barberries kept this year, and I told her they did not keep well at all, for I eat them all up before New-year; and then she laughed, and told me to tell you she had more on hand than she could use till they come round again, and that she would send you a crock of them the first chance she could find."

"Weel! an', indeed, that's varry good uv her. I'll be beholden to her for that same. She is varry kind."

"Yes, indeed, she is; she is just as kind as she can be. Oh, they live so pleasantly, grandmother; they have every thing on that great farm that heart can desire; and they are just like one great family. Old Landlord Nurse—he seemed just like one of the old patriarchs when he stood up to bless the table, with his long, white hair floating over his shoulders—dear old man !

"But, grandmother, I have got some queer news to tell you. Don't you remember what we heard about those children and girls at Mr. Parris's house—how they had meetings there to try tricks and charms, and practice all sorts of black arts ? Don't you remember hearing of it ?"

"Yes, Allie; I mind it. An' I thought it wa' unco' strange doings — at the *Manse, too !*"

"Yes, I know. Well, they have gone on worse and worse—they behave awfully now. The people don't know what to make of it —some say they are crazy, and some think they make it up. Oh ! and they have (or pretend to have, I don't know which it is) terrible fits ; and they will scream and rave, and foam at the mouth, and bleed at the nose, and drop down to the floor as if they were dead, and be cold and stiff ; and they'll declare they see and hear things that no one else can hear or see, and, oh! I can't tell you what they don't do. The neighbors are called in; but no one can do any thing with them. They call them 'the afflicted children.'

"Well, we were talking of it at the table. 'Afflicted children! indeed!—afflicted fiddlesticks, I say,' quoth Goody Nurse; 'I don't believe a word of it; I believe it's all shamming. If either of my little maids had trained on so at their age, I guess I would have afflicted them with the end of my broomstick. I would have whipped it out of them, I know. They have been left to go with them pagan slaves,' she says, 'till their heads are half cracked; and Parson Parris, he just allows and encourages it. If he'd box their ears for them, all round, three times a day, I guess it would cure them,' says she.

"Then Thomas Preston spoke up, and he says: 'I think, Goody, you are too hard on the children. Maybe, if you had seen them, you would feel differently. I have, and it is just awful to behold their fits; and I believe every word of it.'

" ' Well, I don't, son Thomas;' says Goody, ' and that is where you and I differ. If they are sick, I pity them, with all my heart, I'm sure; for nobody knows better than I do what a dreadful thing it is to have fits. I had them once when one of my children was born. But that is no excuse for letting them disturb the whole meeting-house. If they can't behave, let them stay at home, I say. I believe that Mr. Parris is at the bottom of it all; I don't think much of him, and I never did.'

"'Tut! tut! Goody,' said Landlord Nurse. 'Bridle in that unruly little member of thine; it is no use talking of these things, and it is not well to talk against your minister.'

" ' He aint my minister,' says she, again; ' he never was, and never will be, and I'm glad of it. I belong to the Old Church, and I never separated from it, as you know; and I only go to the village church when I can't go to town. I never did like Mr. Parris, even when you, father, and the old committee first gave him a call; and I'm sure, son Tarbell, when you and the young men took the matter into your own hands, and gave him a second call, I always thought you had better have left it where it was, in the hands of your elders. I don't like the man. I won't say he's a bad man, but I don't say he's a good one ; and I, for one, won't go to meeting again while those saucy, impudent girls are allowed to interrupt the worship of the Lord. If it is not silly, it is wicked ; and if it is not wicked, it is silly ; and, any way, I won't go to hear it, I know.'

" Oh, grandmother, I could not but laugh to hear how she did run on ; but Elizabeth, who sat next to me, pulled my sleeve, and whispered me, 'I do wish mother would not talk so ; I feel sure she will get into trouble if she does.'

" ' How so ?' says I.

" ' Why,' she says, ' this is no time to be making enemies ; and somebody may repeat what she says.'

" ' Well,' said I, ' there's nobody here but your own family—and me.'

" ' Oh ! I did not mean the present company,' says she, laughing ; ' but it is just so always. Mother is a dear, good woman as ever lived—she would not hurt a fly ; but she is very outspoken, and there is always an ill bird in the air to catch up such thoughtless words and make the worst of them; and mother is too free—I wish she was not.'

" But, grannie, the girls have got so bold, it seems they don't mind any body; and last Sabbath-day, it seems, they spoke right out in meeting."

" Spoke in meetin'? What, them children spoke in prayer an' exhortation ? Gude save us; did I ever !"

" No, no, grannie; far worse than that. Prayer ? — no, indeed !   Mr. Lawson was to preach that day, and Abigail Williams spoke right out in meeting, and spoke impudently to him. Before he had time to begin, she cried out, 'Come! stand up, and name your text;' and when he had given it, 'That's a long text,' cries she. And then, while he was preaching, another cries out, 'Come! there's enough of that,' and more like that. Was it not shameful? And they said Ann Putnam was so rude that the people next her in the seatings had to hold her down by main force. Goody Nurse said it was shameful that Mr. Parris did not interfere and stop them, and I think so. too. But, as she said, if the minister allowed it, who could venture to do any thing to stop them ?

" So then they sent for Dr. Griggs (his niece, Elizabeth Hubbard, is one of them), and he could not make out what ailed them; and he said he thought they must be bewitched !

" And Mr. Parris has had a meeting of all the neighboring ministers at his own house; and they talked to the children, and prayed over them; but they did not get any satisfaction. And now they all say the children are bewitched. Goody Nurse says she don't believe a word of it, and that Mr. Parris ought to have stopped it at once, in the first of it, as he might easily have done. She said he was not her minister, and she was glad he was not; but if he had been, she would not go, to have such a shameful disturbance.

" And now, grannie, they all believe the children are bewitched ; and every one is asking, ' Who can it be ? Who are the witches that make all this trouble ?' And nobody knows. Why, is it not an awful thing ? Grandmother, do you believe it ?"

" Whist, Allie, I canna tell; the De'il is fu' of a' subtlety."

" But are there really any witches now, grannie ?"

" I dinna ken, lassie. I mind me at hame, I used to hear tell o' fairies an' kelpies an' warlocks ; an' wha' for nae witches? Gude be betune us an' harm ! Dinna talk of sic' things, my bairn ; it's nae good to be naming them. Gude be aroun' us this night an' foriver ! Get ye out the Bible, my lassie, an' read us the prayers."

" Not yet, grandmother ; it's early yet."

" Niver ye mind if it is, Allie. Yer tongue ha' rin on sae fast syne ye come in that my old head is fairly upset, and I'd fain gae to my bed ; an' I'm sure ye maun be weel tired with yer lang walk yersel'. Sae bring the guid book, an' ca' in Winny."

And Allie brought out the big Bible, summoned old Winny, and reverently read the service for the day, the prayers, a hymn, and a chapter from the New Testament ; and so closed the, to her, eventful day.

CHAPTER IV.

THE GATHERING OF THE STORM.

"Men spake in whispers—each one feared to meet another's eye;
As iron seemed the sterile earth, as brass the sullen sky.
But patience had her perfect work, abundant faith was given;
Oh! who shall say the scourge of earth doth not bear fruit
for heaven?"

S the occurrences at Salem village, of which mention has been made in a previous chapter, and of which Alice Campbell, on her return from Nurse's Farm, had brought the first tidings to her grandmother, were destined to assume an importance far more than commensurate with their apparently trivial beginning; and as "the little cloud scarcely bigger than a man's hand" was afterward to spread and deepen, until its baneful influence overwhelmed for a time the powers of truth, reason, and justice, and the whole land sat trembling in the horror of great darkness, it becomes necessary to the course of our narrative that we should turn back and learn what the pages of history and the voices of tradition have preserved of the commencement of the strange and terrible delusion which, under the name of the "Salem Witchcraft," has made itself known and recognized over more than half the world.

Salem village, subsequently known as Danvers, where the first outbreak of this fearful scourge had its rise, was not in those early days a distinct and independent town: it was then the suburbs, the outgrowth, and the more rural portion of the town of Salem.

It had been the sagacious policy of the infant colony, as soon as possible, to issue grants of large tracts of land to influential men, of independent means, enterprising spirit, and liberal views—such men as Winthrop, Dudley, Browne, Endicott, Bishop, Ingersoll, and others; men who had the power, as well as the will, to lay out roads, subdue the forest, clear the ground, and by introducing the desirable arts of husbandry, call out the productive power of the soil.

Afterward, when these large tracts of land were broken up and subdivided, either among the heirs of the original grantees, or sold in portions to other smaller landowners, the people of "Salem village," or "Salem Farms," as it was often termed, continued to retain and support the character of intelligence, stability, and enterprise which had been acquired from the influence of these early founders and leading minds.

In the course of progressive years, as their population naturally and widely increased, they formed a new parish, being a branch of the mother church at Salem; but their ministerial or parochial affairs do not appear to have been happy.

Their first preacher, the Rev. James Bayley, came to the village church in the year 1671; but his call was not a unanimous one, and much bitter disaffection and rancorous discussion followed it, until Mr. Bayley, despairing of ever conciliating the affections of his contentious flock, left them, and, withdrawing from the ministry, studied the profession of medicine.

His successor in the church, the Rev.

George Burroughs, entered upon his duties
in 1680; but he found the parish in a most
unsettled and irritable state of feeling. The
personal friends of Mr. Bayley—for he had
many strong partisans—concentrated all their
bitterness and hostility upon the head of his
innocent successor; added to this were the
troubled pecuniary relations between him
and his parish, which were never clearly adjusted, and, in sheer despair of ever obtaining
an impartial and fair settlement with his de-
moralized people, he, too, resigned his situation and left the village.

The Rev. Deodat Lawson was the next incumbent. He commenced his ministry in
1684—how long he held it is uncertain; but
he, too, finding it impossible to evoke any
harmony out of the discord in the parish, re-
linquished the situation and removed back
to Boston, being afterward settled at Scitu-
ate, New England.

The next minister (and this brings us to
the period of the witchcraft delusion) was
the Rev. Samuel Parris. Possibly warned
by the fate of his three predecessors, he was
very strict and exacting in making his terms

of settlement. His first call, made by the committee of the church in November, 1688, he held in suspense, failing to respond to it for some months; until the young men of the parish, feeling that their elders were making no advance, took the matter into their own hands, and gave him a second call in April, 1689; and he commenced his duties as their preacher from that time, although not regularly ordained until the close of the year.

Whether owing to the unauthorized interference of the young men, which settled him thus prematurely, or by some intentional and overreaching misconception on the part of Mr. Parris, there sprung up a constant and imbittered discussion as to the terms of his settlement—he maintaining himself to be entitled by the terms of his agreement to the parsonage house and the glebe lands; which the other party maintained to be their inalienable church property, which they had neither the intention nor the power to convey away.

This sharp mercantile spirit, which he constantly betrayed in his perpetual " hig-

gling" about the terms of his salary, and
the harsh and exasperating manner in which
he upon all occasions magnified his office,
checking and restraining the usual powers
of his deacons and elders, had rendered him
thoroughly repugnant to all the preconceived
ideas and feelings of the sensible and independent farmers of Salem village; and he,
on his part, seems to have entertained no
pleasant or friendly feelings toward his
people.

It was under these peculiarly irritating
feelings and circumstances, when ill-temper
and acrimonious discontent and discussion
prevailed on all sides, that the first swell of
the great tidal-wave became perceptible,
which afterward beat down the barriers
of common - sense, and engulfed so many
happy homes in fatal and irremediable woe.

During the winter of 1691 and '92, a party of young girls, about a dozen in number,
were in the habit of meeting together at
Mr. Parris's house; their names, as they have
come down to us, are:

Elizabeth Parris, aged 9—the daughter of
the minister.

Abigail Williams, aged 11—a niece of Mr. Parris, and residing in his family.

Ann Putnam, aged 12—daughter of Thomas Putnam, the parish clerk.

Mary Walcott, aged 17—daughter of Deacon Jonathan Walcott.

Mercy Lewis, aged 17—servant in the family of John Putnam, constable.

Elizabeth Hubbard, aged 17—niece of Mrs. Dr. Griggs, and living in her family.

Elizabeth Booth, aged 18.

Susannah Sheldon, aged 18.

Mary Warren, aged 20—servant in the family of John Proctor.

Sarah Churchill, aged 20—servant to George Jacobs, Senior.

Three young married women—Mrs. Ann Putnam, mother of the above-named girl, a Mrs. Pope, and Mrs. Bibber; to these must be added the names of John Indian and Tituba, his wife, slaves in the family of Mr. Parris, and brought by him from the Spanish West Indies, where he had been engaged in trade before entering the ministry.

For what definite and avowed purpose these meetings at the house of the pastor had originally been intended, we have no information; but their ultimate purpose seems to have been to practice sleight of hand, legerdemain, fortune-telling, sorcery, magic, palmistry, necromancy, ventriloquism, or whatever in more modern times is classed under the general name of Spiritualism.

During the course of the winter, they had become very skillful and expert in these unholy arts. They could throw themselves into strange and unnatural attitudes; use strange exclamations, contortions, and grimaces; utter incoherent and unintelligible speech. They would be seized with fearful spasms or fits, and drop as if lifeless to the ground; or, writhing as if in agony of insufferable tortures, utter loud screams and fearful shrieks, foaming at the mouth or bleeding from the nose.

It should be borne in mind that the actors in these terrible scenes were for the most part young girls, at the most nervous and impressible period of life—a period when a too rapid growth, over-study, over-exertion, or various other predisposing causes, are often productive of hysteria, hypochondria, and nervous debility, which, if not met and counteracted by judicious care, has often tended to insanity, and

> "The delicate chain
> Of thought, once tangled, never cleared again."

Let it be remembered, too, that these misguided young persons had been engaged for long months in studies of the most wild and exciting nature, unlawful and unholy, and in the practice of all forbidden arts—studies and practices under the unhallowed influences of which the strongest and most stolid of maturer minds might well have been expected to break down; that they had been in daily and hourly communication with John Indian and Tituba, the two Spanish West Indian slaves — creatures of the lowest type, coarse, sensual, and ignorant—who had been their companions, teachers, and leaders, indoctrinating them in all the pagan lore, hideous superstitions, and revolting ceremonials of their own idolatrous faith, and is it to be wondered at if their weak reason tottered and reeled in the fearful trial? If they were not mad would be the greater wonder.

But these things could not be enacted in a little quiet village and not be known; nor was it intended they should be. And, attention being called to their strange condition and unaccountable behavior, the whole wondering neighborhood was filled with consternation and pity at the unwonted proceedings; from house to house the strange tidings spread with wonderful rapidity, and gaining doubtless at every repetition; and no attempt at concealment being made, but, on the contrary, rather an ostentatious display of the affair, crowds flocked together from every quarter to see and listen and wonder in horror and amazement.

No explanation of the mystery was given, and, excited by the attention they received and the wonder they attracted, the children, emulating each other in their strange accomplishments, grew worse and worse, until the whole community became excited and aroused to a most intense degree. Every thing else was forgotten or set aside, and there was no other topic of thought or conversation; and finding themselves the objects of universal attention, " the observed of all observers," the girls were roused by ambition to new manifestations of the extraordinary power they were influenced by, and outdid all they had done before.

At last, as no change for the better occurred, Dr. Grigg, the village physician, was sent for. He was the uncle by marriage of one of the girls, and possibly not quite an impartial judge in the matter, and after an examination — or we might better say an exhibition on the part of the girls—he declared his medical skill at fault, and pronounced his grave and deliberate opinion that the children were *bewitched.*

This was not an uncommon conclusion in those days; for a superstitious belief in demonology was a commonly received thing, and any symptoms not common, or not referable to commonly understood natural causes, were usually attributed to the influence of " an evil eye." Finding (possibly to their own surprise) that their magical pretensions were thus gravely indorsed and upheld by medical science, " the afflicted children," as they were now termed, grew more bold and proceeded to greater lengths—often disturbing the exercises of prayer-meetings and the services of the sanctuary.

On one Sabbath-day, when Mr. Lawson was to preach, before he had time to commence, one of the girls, Abigail Williams, the niece of Mr. Parris, rudely called out to him, "Come, stand up, and name your text;" and when he had given it, she insolently replied, "That is a long text." And during the sermon, another of them impudently called out, "Come, there is enough of that." And again, as the no doubt .disconcerted speaker referred to the point of doctrine he had been endeavoring to expound, the same insolent voice called out to him, "I did not know you had any doctrine; if you did, I have forgotten it." While yet another became so riotous and noisy that the persons near her in the "seatings," as they were termed, had to hold her down to prevent the services being wholly broken up.

As the girls were regarded with mingled pity and consternation, as being the helpless victims of some terrible and supernatural power, they were not punished or reprimanded; and as they were some of them members of the minister's own family, and he did not seem to dare to check or blame them, it was of course to be understood that he countenanced and believed in the strange influence under which they professed to be suffering, and of course his belief governed that of many of his congregation.

But all were not so compliant of faith. Several members of the Nurse family and others openly manifested their strong disapprobation of such desecration of the Lord's house and the Lord's day, and declared their intention of absenting themselves from attendance on the Sabbath services while such a state of things was allowed; and it was afterward noticed that whosoever did this was sure to be marked out as an object of revenge.

In the mean time fasts and prayer-meetings were resorted to in private families for the restoration of the afflicted ones and the subjugation of the power of the Evil Spirit, who, as the great enemy of souls, was believed to have come among them. All this heightened and helped on the terrible popular excitement, and Mr. Parris convened an assemblage of all the neighboring ministers to meet at his own house, and devote the day to solemn supplication to the Divine Power to rescue them from the power of Satan.

This reverend body of the clergy came, saw the children, questioned them, and witnessed their unaccountable behavior, and, struck dumb with astonishment at what they heard and saw, declared their belief that it must be and was the power of the Evil One.

This clerical opinion was at once made known, and, as it coincided with the medical opinion of Dr. Grigg, it was considered conclusive. No doubt could withstand such an irresistible array of talent, and horror and dire fanaticism ruled the hour. Society was broken up, business was suspended, men looked at each other in unspoken suspicion, and excited crowds gathered to witness the awful workings of the devil, or bear the exaggerated tidings from house to house.

Up to this time it is possible—nay, even more, it seems probable—that the miserable authors of this terrible excitement had·had no clearly defined intention or even perception of the awful sin to the commission of which their deeds were rapidly leading them; they had begun in sport, or at best without consideration—in a spirit, it might be, of unholy curiosity and merry malice; possibly the widespread notoriety they had attracted would, at the first, have more than satisfied their ambition. It is doubtful to what extent they had learned to believe in their own pretensions; but they had gone too far to retrace their steps, even if they had wished to do so; the feverish excitement around them carried them along with it; they had " sowed the whirlwind, and they must reap the storm." If they had any misgivings, any doubts of their own demoniac power, the full, free faith in it expressed by all around them may have confirmed their own wavering belief, called out into force their unholy ambition, and overwhelmed every better and more human feeling.

Up to this time they had accused no one as the author of their sufferings; but it was the common and universally received doctrine or belief that the devil could not act upon mortals, or in mortal affairs, by his own immediate and direct power, but only through the agency of human beings who were in confederacy with him; and now the question naturally arose on all sides, "Who are the devil's agents in this work? who is it thus afflicting these children? There must be some one among us who is thus acting—and who is it?"

No one could tell. Men looked around them with hungry eyes, eager to trace the devil's agents; and the question was pressed home upon the girls by every one, "If you *are* thus tormented—if you are pricked with pins, and pinched, and beaten, and choked, and strangled—tell us who it is that does it; surely you must know—tell us, then, who it is that has thus bewitched you."

Thus importuned on every hand, they could no longer withstand the pressure; their power was at stake, and their sinful ambition forbade them to recant.

Timidly at first they breathed out their terrible accusations; unconscious it may be then of the death-dealing nature of their words, they named three persons — Sarah Good, Sarah Osburn, and the slave woman Tituba—as the persons who thus afflicted them.

The children were inimitable actors; they were well trained, and had studied their parts carefully; their acting was perfect, but it would seem there must have been a master-mind acting as prompter and stage-manager; had there been no other evidence of this concealed, maturer mind, the wonderful sagacity with which they selected these first victims must have forced the conviction upon us.

Sarah Good was an object of prejudice in the village; her husband had deserted her; she was a poor, forlorn, destitute creature of ill-repute, without any regular home, begging her way from door to door; one for whom no one cared, and whom no one would regret. Sarah Osburn was a poor, sick creature; she, too, was unhappy in her domestic relations; care and grief had worn her; she was bedridden, and depressed in mind, if not actually distracted; she, too, was an easy victim. The third, Tituba, was the master-stroke of the policy—as her having been one of their own number would disarm suspicion, while it could be so arranged at the examination as to confirm their power.

Warrants were immediately made out and .issued against the persons thus named, for by this time a conviction of the reality of the sufferings of the girls, and that they were the result of witchcraft, was nearly universal among the people.

Great pains were taken to give notoriety and scenic effect to these first examinations; possibly it was thought that by taking up the matter with a high hand they should strike terror to the Evil One and his confed-erates, and stamp out the power of Satan at once and forever.

·A special court was therefore at once convened to meet and hold its first session at Salem village on the first of March, for the trial of the persons thus accused of this strange and monstrous crime; and in the mean time the unhappy prisoners were lodged in jail, loaded with fetters and chains (it being the commonly received opinion that mere mortal hemp had not sufficient power to bind a witch), there to abide "in durance vile" the sitting of the court which was to investigate the strange charges brought against them, and to decide the question of their guilt or innocence.

CHAPTER V.

"As the Greegree holds his Fetish from the white man's gaze
    apart."

IT was just at the close of a sultry and
oppressive day, when the heavily
lowering clouds, the deep, low muttering of the distant thunder, and
the sharp, but infrequent flashes of lightning,
told of the gathering tempest which was
slowly rolling up the darkening heavens,
that a man, issuing from the back door of
the Rev. Mr. Parris's house, made his way
silently and under cover of the deepening
twilight through the straggling street of
Salem village.

This man was "Indian John," as he was
usually called, a domestic slave in the service of Mr. Parris, then minister of the little
church gathered at the village.

We have said that the man was a slave,

but he was not an African slave; he was supposed to be from one of the Spanish West India Islands, or the adjacent mainlands of Central or South America; he and his wife Tituba having been brought to the colony by Mr. Parris, who had been engaged in commercial traffic in Barbadoes before he entered the ministry and became pastor of the village church.

The early church records show that Mr. Parris was not a universally popular incumbent of the office which he held; the mercenary and haggling bargain he had driven with the church committee, in regard to the terms of his salary, represents him to us as having more of the spirit of the sharp and overreaching trader than the urbane gentleman or zealous Christian; but at present we have little to do with the character of the master—it is with the movements of the slave that we are now concerned.

We have already stated that John and Tituba were not Africans, and the difference which marked them from the few African slaves then in the colony was much to the disadvantage of the Spaniards. The real

African is usually gentle in temperament, and even in his lowest type of development has almost always an honest face; there is no look of concealment or hidden purpose in the large, confiding, open eye—open almost too far for comeliness, but still reassuring in its absence of all latent treachery. The dusky face of the African bears usually one of two several expressions—either a patient look of infinite and hopeless sadness, or a frank, reckless lightheartedness, breaking out into thoughtless jollity.

The faces of the two West Indian slaves were full as dusky, but far more repellent; traces of their fierce Spanish blood and temperament lurked in their long, narrow, vicious, half-shut eyes, which flashed their keen, malignant glances from beneath the heavy hanging eyelids; the swarthy lowering brow was narrow and retreating, and the whole lower portion of the face was sensuous in the extreme, the coarse, heavy, powerful jaws having the ferocity of the beast of prey, united to the low cunning of the monkey.

Having passed down the street to the

very extremity of the village, ostentatiously speaking to several persons on his way, as if to enable him to prove an alibi if his future course should be traced, John suddenly turned aside, and, doubling on his track like a hunted hare, he made his escape by tortuous windings from the village, and proceeded at a rapid sort of dog-trot to the woods, where the unbroken forest stretched its primeval shade nearest to the infant settlement.

Hurrying along beneath the starless, leaden skies, with the unerring instinct of a brute nature, he made his way over hill and dale, over bushes, rocks, briars, and quaking morass, until, having entered the intricacies of the forest, he reached a lonely spot, where a spur of the low, wooded hills lay between him and the little settlement he had just quitted.

Here he paused for a moment, and took a rapid but keen survey of the place. Apparently he was right—his memory or his instinct had not been at fault; he measured the space with earnest gaze, then silently, in the dim light, he walked up to a small group of trees, and passed his hand up the smooth trunks, one by one, as high as his hand could reach—one—two—three he has felt, and passed them by; at the fourth he halted—ah! he has found it—his hand had encountered the "blaze," or notch, cut in the bark of the tree; this was the place he sought.

Hastily scraping away the fallen leaves and dead branches of a former year from the roots of the tree, he drew from his pocket a small spaddle, or trowel, and commenced to dig an oblong cavity about the shape and size of an infant's grave. Evidently the ground had been dug before, for it offered little resistance to his efforts; but still the labor was sufficiently exhaustive, combined with the close, sultry breathlessness of the night, to bring large drops of perspiration from his dusky brow. But the heavy beads of moisture dropped unheeded to the ground; he never for them remitted his absorbing labor.

A slight rustle of the brushwood, and beneath the black shadow of the trees a stealthy step is furtively approaching; but it does not startle him—he was expecting it. It was Tituba, his wife, who like himself had been baffling observation to join him at the rendezvous. They looked at each other, but no word passed between them. On her dark face was expressed inquiry; on his, as he looked down at his work, she read the answer.

Then Tituba began busily gathering together small dry twigs of wood, bits of bark, and fir cones, and built them up, placing them in order as for a small fire, rejecting all larger wood as unsuitable for her purpose; and when this was done, she came to her husband's side, squatting down, like a hideous toad, by the brink of the hole which he was digging—sitting upon her haunches, with her knees drawn up, her elbows resting upon them, and her spread hands supporting her heavy jaws on either side. So she sat, motionless but intent, her snaky eyes never moving from the spot, until John, having reached the object of his search, lifted out something wrapped up in coarse foreign mats.

Removing the coverings, he brought to

view a hideous wooden figure—an idol, probably — bearing a mocking and frightful resemblance to a human being. This figure
was about two feet high, of ghastly ugliness,
and coarsely bedaubed with red and blue
paint.

Freeing the figure from its mats, John
proceeded to set it up before the face of the
rock, and behind the little bonfire which
Tituba had heaped up; and then, rubbing
some bits of dry wood rapidly together, he
procured a fire, and lighted a blaze. Join-
ing their hands together to form a ring, the
two next danced silently round the slowly
igniting fire, with mad leaps and strange,
savage contortions of limb and features, until the whole mass was in a blaze, and the
red flames threatened to consume them. Then
they unclasped their hands, and Tituba drew
forth from the bosom of her dress some gums,
herbs, and spices of pungent, acrid odor,
and flung them onto the fire, and, making a
rude sort of besom of broken green branches, she fanned the rising smoke and curling
flames into the grinning face of the idol;
while John took from his bosom a small

new-born pup, and, coolly severing the head of the blind and unresisting little victim, held the body above the flames, and let the blood drip over the hissing embers. Next the woman (forgive me, oh! ye of the softer sex) drew from the folds of her dress some rough wooden puppets, or effigies, bearing as much resemblance to human beings as do our modern clothes-pins; one by one she held them up silently before her husband's face, who regarded them gravely, and nodded to each one in succession, as if he had recognized or named it, and, as he did so, she thrust them one by one into the circling flames.

By this time it was nearly dark; a low, sobbing wind began to sweep among the branches, and the first great heavy drops of the approaching thunder-shower fell at distant intervals.

Then they both simultaneously threw themselves upon their knees, resting their foreheads upon the ground, while their hands were clasped, and extended upon the earth far beyond their heads—much as in pictures of the Syrian deserts we see pilgrims prostrating themselves before the terrible sirocco; and now for the first time they broke silence by giving utterance to a wild, low incantation.

It was a rude sort of rhythmical recitative, of alternate parts—first one and then the other, rising upon their knees and sitting back upon their heels, with brawny arms held out to the frowning heavens, would utter their fiendish jargon in some strange pagan tongue, to which the deep bass of the prolonged and rolling thunder lent a fearful accompaniment; and still, at the close of every thunder-peal, the demon-like performers answered it with fierce peals of mocking, idiot laughter.

But at length the unhallowed flame has burned itself out, and the devil worship is ended. John Indian enveloped the image in its mats, and laid it back into its grave; and, while he covered it up again with earth, Tituba stamped out the remaining embers and scattered them. With infinite care, the two performers in these awful rites gathered up twigs and branches and scattered them about, so as to conceal all traces of their presence, and then together they began their homeward way.

By this time the storm was down upon them in all its awful fury: great trees creaked and groaned beneath the biting blasts of the wind; huge branches, torn off, obstructed their way; hail and rain smote their uncovered heads and wet their shivering bodies to the skin; the rattling thunder leaped from hill to hill, and sheets of blue, fiery lightning blazed around them; but they never wavered, never swerved from their direct way.

Plunging on in the same blind instinct which enables the dull ox to find his owner's crib, or the ravenous beast of prey to reach its lair, they made their unseen way to the village; and when, half an hour later, the Rev. Mr. Parris returned from the prayer-meeting which he had convened for the benefit of "the afflicted children," John was ready at his post to take his master's horse, and Tituba opened the door for him as usual.

Whether the demon rites of the avowed Pagan or the prayers of the professing Christian were more acceptable to the dread powers to which they were severally addressed is a question which Time may indeed ask, but which Eternity alone can answer.

CHAPTER V.

THE PLEDGE OF FRIENDSHIP.

"A place in thy memory, dearest,
   Is all that I claim;
To pause and look back when thou hearest
   The sound of my name.

"As the young bride remembers her mother,
   Whom she loves, though she never may see;
As the sister remembers her brother—
   So, dear one! remember thou me."

ONE fine spring day, shortly after Alice's visit to Nurse's Farm, she had wandered in the early afternoon down to the sea-shore, and stood awhile idly looking out over the quiet water. Alice, who still retained all the impulsiveness of her childish days, and was still, as then, influenced by every atmospheric change, and sensitively affected by every modification of the many phases of Nature (with whom she lived in terms of the closest intimacy), grew buoyant with delight at the perfect beauty of the day, and drew in with every breath of the pure, sweet air a positive enjoyment from the very sense of life, youth, and health.

There was not breeze enough to ruffle the surface of the sea; and the calm water lay, softly pulsating at her feet, so still and clear that the intense lapis-lazuli blue of the sky, and its soft garniture of fleecy white clouds, was repeated upon its unbroken surface as clearly as in a mirror.

As Alice stood and gazed, her spirits rising within her at the profuse beauty showered all around her, she experienced that almost universal desire for rapid motion which is oftenest expressed in the common words " wanted to fly;" but as that kind of locomotion was then, as now, out of the question, her next thought was naturally of her little boat, which was moored close by.

In a moment, without pause or reflection, she had embarked and rowed gayly from the shore.

Those who love the water are accustomed to speak in ardent terms of the thrilling enjoyment they find in being upon it; it may be in the exultant sense of superiority that they are thus enabled to ride and rule triumphant over an element so limitless, and of a power so immeasurably vast; for the love of dominion is a deep-seated principle in human nature. But, whatever the cause, Alice enjoyed her trip exceedingly; her spirits rose with the accustomed exercise, from which she had been debarred all the winter; and as she plied her oars vigorously and skillfully, bursts of glad girlish laughter, and snatches of sweet old songs —ballads learned far away in the Scottish home of her infancy—floated after her.

She had meant but to take a short pull, just to practice her arms; but the beauty of the day tempted her on farther and farther, and she scarcely paused until she had reached the shore of Marblehead. She did not land there, but turning toward home, rowed a little way, and then, resigning her oars, she reclined lazily in the boat, suffering it to drift slowly homeward on the incoming tide; while she lay building castles in the air, such as youth and idleness are wont to make pleasure-houses of.

But at last a gleam of western brightness

recalled her to the fact that the day was spending; and she suddenly remembered that her grandmother might be uneasy at her prolonged and unexplained absence, and, resuming her oars, she rowed steadily and rapidly back to shore.

As Alice rounded the little headland of Salem Neck, she noticed a small canoe, rowed by two persons, which was hovering afar off on the outer verge of the harbor, and apparently making for the same point as herself.

The little skiff was yet too far distant for even Alice's bright eyes to discern who were its occupants; nor did she give the matter more than a passing thought, for boats and canoes were then the more common mode of transportation — almost every householder owned one, and her own little craft had already been hailed by half a dozen of her towns-people in the course of her afternoon's trip. So, wholly occupied with her own busy thoughts and pleasant fancies, she rowed on, making her way straight to the little landing-place, wholly unobservant that the other boat, propelled by its two rowers, had gained rapidly upon her, and was just in her wake.

Springing lightly on shore, Alice proceeded to fasten her little bark at its usual mooring-place, heedless of the approach of the stranger, until, as she turned round, she suddenly found herself face to face with a stalwart Indian warrior, decked out in all the imposing pomp of his feathers, arms, and war-paint.

For one moment Alice was startled, and doubtless most modern young ladies would have shrieked or fainted at such an appalling encounter—but Alice did neither. She was aware of no enmities, and consequently felt no fear, and she had grown up in friendly acquaintance with many of the better and most civilized of their Indian neighbors; so, although the color did indeed deepen on her transparent cheek, it was less from fear than surprise and maiden modesty at finding herself thus suddenly confronted by a young stranger of the other sex; but, before she had time to analyze her own feelings, the young warrior had spoken.

"Are the memories of the pale faces

indeed so short," he said, in grave, low tones, which, though sad, awakened in Alice dim, pleasant memories of the past, "that the sister does not remember the brother? that the Water-lily has forgotten the Fir-tree?"

"Oh! Pashemet, Pashemet! my brother! welcome, welcome!" cried Alice, impulsively. "Forget? Oh, no! never, never!" and springing forward with extended hands, she placed them both in the hands of the young warrior, and looked up into his face with the sweet, frank, confiding smile of her childhood. "I am so glad! Oh, my brother! I have looked for you so long—I have so longed to see you."

"That is well—that is good!" said the young warrior, gravely, though a flush of gratified feeling rose up even to his dark brow. "The words of the young pale face are good; I, too, have wished to look upon my sweet Water-lily again. Listen to me, my sister—the people of my tribe hold their council-fire not far from this, and I was bidden to it. I came—but I have come more than twenty miles out of my way to look once more upon the face of my little sister; and see—I have brought something to show her."

Turning, even while he spoke, toward the little boat, which was rocking on the water's brim, Pashemet uttered a low, sweet cry, resembling the note of the wood-pigeon, and in quick obedience to his summons, from among the gaudy blankets and glossy furs, which were heaped in gay confusion in one end of the boat, arose a dusky but beautiful young Indian woman. Tall, straight, and supple as a young forest tree, she leaped lightly on shore, and stepping with the free grace of a gazelle to his side, she glided with quiet motion just before him, resting her slight form against his shoulder, and, folding her arms, stood in an attitude of shy yet proud repose; her great, eloquent black eyes, bright as diamonds, stealing quick furtive glances of curiosity and admiration from beneath their drooping, long-lashed lids at the fair young daughter of the pale faces.

"Behold, my sister!" Pashemet said, in a voice of inexpressible tenderness, as he took the little dusky hand of his bride in his, and held it out to Alice. "This is the Silver Fawn; she dwells in your brother's wigwam; she makes his nets; she trims his arrows; she weaves his wampum; she is his sunshine. Will not my sister give her a welcome too?"

"Yes, yes, indeed!" said Alice, cordially. "She is my brother's wife—she is my sister, then. I will love her;" and, taking the offered hand kindly in hers, she bent forward, and pressed a warm, sisterly kiss upon the smooth, round cheek of the dark but beautiful stranger.

"Good!" said the young husband, laconically. "The words of my sister are pleasant. See!"—and as he spoke he took their united hands in both of his own—"See, my sister! we are three, and yet we are but one."

Then, as the two graceful heads bent before him, Pashemet took a small strand of Alice's golden curls, and a strand of his wife's long, raven-black locks, and with quick, dexterous fingers braided them together, and severing the united braid with his hunting-knife, he held it up to Alice, saying, "Behold, my token!" and hid it in the folds of his blanket. "Yet listen again, my sister," he said. "The Great Spirit has smiled in love upon my little Water-lily, and it has blossomed very fair; but my sister has neither father nor brother to take care of her; but see, Pashemet is a boy no longer— he is a man;" he drew himself up proudly as he spoke. "My father is dead. Pashemet is a warrior and a Sagamore now; his arm is strong; his arrows are swift; his young men are braves—they do his bidding. Take this, then," and he slipped a small chain of wampum from the wrist of the Silver Fawn, and held it out to Alice. "If my sister should ever need the aid of Pashemet, let her send him this by a sure hand—by the hand of a Naumkeag—and the heart and the arm of her brother shall not fail her. And now, farewell!"

"Oh, no, no! not farewell. Pashemet, do not go yet—do not leave me yet, my brother. I have so much to say to you. Come up to the house with me—do not go yet. Stay, oh, stay!"

"Farewell!" repeated the Indian, in a

sweet but inflexible tone. "I can not stay. The day is fading fast; soon night will be upon the waters. We have far to row, and the Silver Fawn is with me. Farewell!" and, catching his young bride in his strong arms, he sprang into the little canoe without apparent effort, and with one vigorous push sent it whirling from the shore; and while Alice stood, holding the little wampum chain in her hands, feeling that that was the only proof that the whole visit was not a day-dream, the little boat had passed round the headland, and was already lost to her sight.

Half an hour later, and Alice came into her grandmother's presence, bright and glowing, and flushed with health, exercise, and excitement.

"Why, Alice! my bairn," said the grandmother, glancing up with ill-concealed admiration at the sweet, blooming young face that bent caressingly over her. "Ye hae been lang awa', my bonnie lassie. I mistrust ye are gettin' to be jist a ne'er-do-weel gad-about. I hae missed ye sadly; an' where hae ye been the noo?"

"Guess, grannie, guess. I will give you three chances. See if you can guess."

"Na', na', Allie, my lass, I kin na' guess; I am na' guid at the guessin'. Sure ye wad na' hae been to Nurse's Farm agin sa sune—wad ye?"

"Oh, no, grandmother! Of course I would not go so soon; but I have been quite as far, I think. Ah! you will never guess; I shall have to tell you. I have been out on the water."

"My darlin', an' is that sae?"

"Yes, indeed, I have. I went down to the shore just for a walk, and the water looked so calm and blue, and our boat was so nice (you know Winny cleaned it out for me last week), that I felt as if I must have a little row. You know I have not been out all winter in her, and I meant only to take a little pull, just to limber my arms a little; but the boat was so trim and nice, the day was so fine and still, and the water was so calm, I went on and rowed across to Marblehead."

"To Marblehead? My certies, that wa' a lang pull for the first ane, I'm thinkin'.

Are ye na' tired, an' did ye gae ashore at Marblehead?"

"Oh, no! I only wanted the exercise, and I got it. My arms ache—I am so out of practice of late. It is full time I began again;" and as she spoke Alice pushed up her loose sleeves, and laughingly rubbed her firm, round, white arms.

"But, grandmother, dear, I have a great adventure to tell you. I have seen Pashemet! only think!"

"Seen Pashemet? Lord save us! Is the lassie wad or fou? An' where wad ye hae seen him?"

Then Alice told her little story of the visit, adding, laughingly, "And, oh, grandmother, grandmother! only think—he is married! Pashemet is married."

"Weel, an' why should na' he be?" And the matron glanced anxiously in her darling's face, as if she half feared to read a disappointment there. "He wa' a braw chiel an' a bonnie laddie; an' I'm gey glad to hear't, giv he ha' gotten a guid, sinsible lassie for his wife."

"Oh, she is a beauty!" said Alice, warmly; "and he seemed so fond of her; and was it not kind in him to bring her here for me to see her? Oh! my dear old friend; Pashemet, my brother. Oh, I am so glad he has got somebody to love him!" And the clear, smiling, truthful blue eyes, looking full into her own, satisfied the grandmother that her unowned fear was misplaced.

"Allie," she said, laughing, "an' do ye mind the day an' ye wa' but an idle wean, an' he fished ye up out o' the water, an' brought ye hame to me on his bock?"

"Do I remember it? To be sure I do. I should be ungrateful indeed if I could ever forget it. It was all my own carelessness too. I remember it as well as if it were but yesterday it happened. I reached too far over the boat to get a water-lily I wanted; and I not only went over myself, but I upset the boat. I shall never forget how I went down, down, down—it seemed as if I should never reach the bottom; and then I saw Pashemet coming down after me, like a great fish-hawk; and he picked me up, and swam ashore with me. I was thoroughly frightened for once in my life; and then the question was how I should get home, for my clothes were so wet I could not move in them ; and at last the great, strong, kind fellow set me on his shoulder, and marched home with me, as if I had been only a wild turkey. Oh! I'll never forget that."

"An' I'll never forgit the droll figure ye made, the twa o' ye, all drouket an' drippin', an' the varry life half scart out of ye! An' he scart half to death aboot ye."

"Well! he saved my life — dear, kind, brave old Pashemet! I'll never forget it while that life remains."

"An' noo, Alice, hear to me : I hae had a visitor too, a' my lane," said Mistress Campbell.

"You don't say so! Have you, indeed? And who was it?—John English's wife?

"Na', na'! not a bit o' it; mine wa' a young mon, too. Ye kinna hae them a' to yersel'—it wa' jist Thomas Preston fra' the Farm. He came to bring the pot o' barberries that Goody Nurse promised ye she'd send ; an' a big pot it is. She's a free han' at the givin', I'm thinkin'. An' he brought ye some flowers that his wife sint ye—them

yellow daffy-down-dillies ye wa' speakin'
aboot. I jist pu' them in a beaker of water
out yander, till ye could settle them; I am
nae hand at it, ye ken."

"How kind they are: I never saw such
people; they remember every thing, and
seem to love to give."

"I'd think sae indeed! an' there's mair
yet. Goody Nurse sint her luve to ye, an'
bid him say ye wa' pleased wi' her fowl;
an' she'd a rooster an' three hins for ye, if
ye could manage to fix a place to keep them
in; an' I said I wa' thinkin' ye could."

"My goodness! find a place for them? I
guess I will, if they have to roost in my own
chamber. I guess Winny and I can fix up
a coop for them somewhere—and won't it
be splendid? Oh! such dear little, fluffy,
yellow chicks as she had. Why, there's no
end to the pleasure I'll have in them. Dear,
kind, generous old Goody! Is she not just
as good and kind as she can be?"

"Whist! Alice, whist! or I'll be gettin'
half jealous o' her mysel'."

"You have no need to be," said the girl,
fondly kissing her. "But I do think she is
too kind to me."

"She is unco' ginerous, surely; an' sae I telled Goodman Preston mysel'. 'She ha' a free han' at the givin',' quo' I. ''Deed ha' she,' says he. 'I dinna think,' he says, 'the Lord ever made a better or kinder woman than Mother Nurse. An' as to givin',' he says, 'Why, we say at hame she'd give awa' the varry ears fra' her head, gin they wad kim off, an' any bodie wanted them.'"

"I almost think she would," said Alice, laughing. "But is he not pleasant? I am sorry I missed him."

"Varry pleasant—an unco' nice young mon. I wanted him to bide here till ye kim hame, but he said he could na'. He had business in the toon, he said, an' he must awa'. But he sat an hour or so, I think, an' he telled me mair about the terrible doin's at the village. Hey, sirs! but it's jist awfu'!"

"What did he tell you about it, grandmother? Do tell me what he said."

"Oh! Lord save us! he says it's dreadfu'. He ha' been to see the childer, an' he says that he believes in them, though most of the family o'er at the Farm doubt them. But he says they hae na' been to see them, an’ they kinna be judge. He says they wi’ fa’ to the floor, as if they were deed, jist; an’ then they wi’ hae sich awfu’ fits. They wi’ foam an’ bleed at the mou’, and they wi’ be a’ knotted up, as it were; an’ whiles their han’s are clenched sae tight, nae ane kin open them; an’ other whiles they are open, an’ stretched out sae stiff nabodie kin bend them; an’ he says it’s jist gruesom’ an’ awfu’ to hear how they’ll groan an’ scriech. An’ sometime they’ll be struck wi’ blindness a’ o’ a sudden, an’ grope aboot, an’ their eyes wide open too. An’ again they’ll cry out they are tormentit; that some ane is stabbin’ them wi’ pins, or bitin’, or pinchin’, or chockin’ them; an’ they’ll gasp for breath, maybe, an’ turn black in the face, an’ ye’d say they wa’ deeing jist. Oh! Lord’s sake! it wa’ jist dreadfu’ to hear him tellin’ it, let alone seein’ it. An’ the folks say they maun be bewitched.”

“And do you believe they are, grannie?”

“Gude sake! an’ how should I ken? I hae na’ seen them, na mair than yersel’.”

“But, if they are bewitched, grannie, who do they think it is that bewitches them?”

"Ah! tha' is what every bodie is spierin' at them, to tell who it is."

"But surely they must know; if any one pinches them, or sticks pins into them, they must know who does it."

"True for ye, Alice! an' I put it to him mysel' that way; an' he said there were twa persons who were suspectit; twa who they hae named—an' who do ye think is ane o' them?"

"I am sure I can not guess. Nobody we know, of course."

"'Deed thin, an' it is too. Alice, do you mind Sarah Good?"

"Sarah Good? No, I think not. I do not remember ever to have heard of her."

"Yes, ye do; certies! Dinna ye mind the puir creature tha' kim beggin' wi' her child, an' ye gave her yer fustian gown an' petticoat, an' I gave her my old shawl an' my black cardinal. Ye mind her, Alice, surely?"

"Yes, indeed! I remember the woman and the child; but I had forgotten the name. But, grandmother, she can not be a witch, I'm sure; I do not believe a word of it—not

E

a single word.   A poor, sick, miserable creature—a 'ne'er-do-weel,' as you may call her, I dare say she might be—a poor, half-crazy, homeless beggar; but I guess she was nothing worse.   And what power can that poor creature have?   If she had any, I think she would have used it to clothe herself and that poor, half-starved child.   Should not you?"

"I dinna ken.   He said the gals charged it upon her, ony way."

"I don't believe it.   But who was the other?   You said there were two."

"I guess ye dinna ken o' the ither.   It is ane Sarah Osburn.   I hae heard tell o' her: she wa' the Widow Prince, a woman o' some substance here once, an' she married her ain farmer mon.   He wa' a Redemptioner, I think they ca' them.   He an' her sons had trouble atween them, an' he left her, an' she ha' been half dementit ever sin'.   I thought sure an' certain she wa' deed long ago; I dinna hear o' her this mony a day; an' noo it turns up she is charged wi' bein' a witch. The gals cry out on her, an' say she is the ane that torments them.   I dinna see how it can be—a puir, feckless old bodie; what power ha' she?"

"But did Goodman Preston believe it?"

"Weel! he did na' jist say; he thinks the sufferings of the gals is real; but he did na' let out his min' aboot the ithers."

"And what are they going to do about it, grandmother?"

"There's a deal to be done aboot it. He said the folks is goin' to get out warrants, an' hae the twa arrested for bein' witches; an' there's to be a court held at the village —a 'special court,' I think he ca'd it (whatsoever that may be, I dinna ken)—an' he says they wi' be tried for their lives for it."

"And what will be done to them if they are found guilty?"

"Gude sake! I dinna ken; an' I did na' ask him. He says the folks at the village are all up in arms like aboot it. They say the devil ha' broken out upon them, an' the people are half beside themselves wi' the terror—runnin' hither an' yon, an' crowds comin' to see the gals' terrible actions; an' ivery bodie talkin' an' spierin' aboot it, an' spreadin' it fra' house to house. But, he says, happen the court kin get to the bottom o' it; an' he hopes it will, an' he prays

they may know, an' be able to put an end
to it; for there's nae doin' ony business, ivery bodie is so cast up about it. Is na' it
awfu'?"

"But I wonder if sensible people there believe in it? Did he say?"

"He did, then. He said Nathaniel Ingersoll, Mr. Parris, an' Joseph Hutchinson, an'
Edward an' Thomas Putnam, they all believed in it. Oh! wae is me! wae is me!
'Deed, but I think it's jist awfu'! awfu'!"

"And you believe it too, then—do you,
grandmother?"

"I dinna ken what to believe, lassie! I
kinna say I do believe in it, an' yet, as folks
say, 'Where there's sae much smoke, there
maun be some fire.'"

"I know. But then, these two poor old
creatures—what power can they possibly
have? Grandmother, I don't think I believe
one word of it."

"Weel-a-weel! I kinna say. But there,
lassie, rin awa' noo; an' dinna fash ony mair
aboot it, for it makes me sick wi' fear."

"But stay a moment, grannie, and tell me
just this one thing: If the devil hath such

power, hath not the Lord our God the greater power?"

"True for ye, lassie! Ye are right; I believe that; an' sure we maun put our trust in Him. But dinna talk mair aboot it noo, for it makes me sair sick at heart; an' I wad fain try to forget it."

CHAPTER VII.

THE FIRST EXAMINATIONS.

"Oh! what were we,
If the All Merciful should mete to us
With the same rigorous measure wherewithal
Sinner to sinner metes? But God beholds
The secrets of the heart—therefore His name
Is—Merciful."

AS this does not purport to be definitely a work upon Witchcraft, it is not our intention to weary the patience or harrow up the feelings of the reader unnecessarily by portraying the painful details of the several trials, except in so far as they have a connection with or a bearing upon the several personages of our story.

The terrible episode of poor Giles Corey we have therefore intentionally omitted—his brave "*contumacy*," as it was then called—the constancy with which he maintained his pertinacious silence, steadfastly refusing to plead, that he might thus preserve to his unfortunate family the little patrimony which he well knew his attainder as a wizard would surely confiscate — his indomitable fortitude under his terrible sufferings, and his heroic death, are all too painful and revolting in their details for admission into such a work as this. If such information is desired, it is matter of history, and may easily be obtained from reliable sources.

But we have thought that by presenting a few passages, taken from the records of the preliminary examination of the persons first accused, and brought up for trial, the reader would gain a clearer realization of the unfairness of the whole proceedings; and see how, owing to the inflamed state of the popular mind, and the preconceived prejudices of all classes of people, clearly including judges and jurors, against the accused, the unhappy prisoners were, in fact, already judged and condemned even before they were brought to trial.

Great pains had been taken to give publicity and *éclat* to the coming event: the session of the court was made the universal subject of thought and conversation; the news was industriously spread far and wide; and persons from all directions flocked together to witness and share in the unfamiliar and exciting scenes.

The strange nature of the whole proceedings—the monstrous and supernatural crime which was to be the object of inquiry and judgment — had roused the people to the wildest curiosity, and this curiosity was heightened and intensified by the universal terror.

There was a solemn romance, a fascination about this great and unfamiliar crime, which lesser and more common offenses, such as arson and petty larceny, could not boast; and then crime of all kinds was less common than now.

We, who live in an age when the public journals collect and daily serve up to us all the crimes of all the world (a very doubtful good, certainly!)—we, to whom murder and suicide seem almost the common road out of life — to whom fatal accidents and wholesale manslaughter are such constantly recurring trivialities that a whole page of them does not destroy our appetite for break-fast—can perhaps form no adequate idea of the mingled awe and curiosity with which our unsophisticated predecessors looked forward to this great event.

The quiet village was therefore thronged with eager strangers, in addition to its own excited population, when, in the morning of the first of March, 1692, the two leading and most distinguished magistrates of the neighborhood, Justices John Hathorne and Jonathan Corwin—who are described as "men of note and influence, whose fathers had been among the first founders of the settlement, and who were assistants, that is, members of the highest legislative and judicial body in the colony, combining the functions of a senate with those of a court of last resort, with most comprehensive jurisdiction"—entered the village. There is no doubt that these distinguished men magnified their office — no doubt it was their purpose and intention so to do; their object undoubtedly was to make the prestige of their authority felt and recognized as a terror to evil-doers; and we may imagine the mighty stir and excitement their arrival was calculated to produce in the primitive little community as they rode into the village with great pomp and ceremony, adorned with all the imposing regalia of their high office, and followed by the long train of. their subordinates and satellites—aids, marshals, and constables—in full force.

Dismounting, they at once proceeded, with such slow haste as the nature of the case called for—with grave severity of countenance, and ominous dignity of step and action, availing themselves of all the awe-inspiring forms of the law, then even more cumbersome in its ceremonial observances than now—to the meeting-house, which was already crowded to its utmost capacity by a dense and excited multitude, who were filled at once with mingled horror of the accused, pity for the accusers, awe of the judges, and curiosity to behold the strange and intensely interesting proceedings of the court.

Here arrangements had already been made to render the meeting-house suitable for the great occasion to which it was now to be put; a raised platform or staging had been erected, on which to place the prisoners in full view, but removed from contact with the spectators; a separate place had been set apart for the accusers, and seats had been placed for the magistrates in front of the pulpit, and facing the people. After the magistrates had with much ceremony been ushered in and taken their appointed seats, the formal announcement was made that the court was now open, and ready to commence the examinations at once.

After prayer had been offered by one of the attending ministers, the constable produced the body of Mrs. Sarah Good, and placed her upon the stand.

If the case had not been such a solemn one, involving life or death, there must have been something almost laughably absurd in the palpable disproportion between the pitiful prisoner, on the one hand, and the array of learning, law, and evidence gathered against her upon the other.

She was a small, weak, miserable creature; a poor, helpless, friendless woman — worn down by a life of want and misery; a homeless vagrant, without character or subsistence; one for whom no one cared, whose perennial pauperism had outworn the patience of nearly all her benefactors, and whose name, if not positively evil, was not respectable — an abject thing to be pitied, not persecuted.

We shall endeavor to give her examination according to the minutes which have been preserved; but let it be remembered that this examination was in the form of questions put to her by Justice Hathorne, evidently expressive of his belief in her guilt, and in the truth of the evidence brought by " the afflicted girls " against her; that no friend or counsel was allowed her; that she was very ignorant, wholly unused to such a cross-examination as she was subjected to, totally unaware of the danger of being entrapped in her unguarded answers, or that what she might say in her wild, random replies was liable to be misunderstood or misrepresented.

Justice Hathorne commenced the examination as follows:

"Sarah Good, what evil spirit have you familiarity with ?"

To which the prisoner responded, " None !"

"Have you made no contracts with the devil ?"

" No! I have not; I never did."

" Why do you hurt these children ?"

" I do not hurt them; I scorn it."

" Who do you employ, then, to do it ?"

" I employ nobody."

" What creature do you employ then ?"

" No creature; but I am falsely accused."

" Why did you go away muttering from Mr. Parris his door ?"

" I did not mutter; but I thanked him for what he gave my child."

" Have you made no contract with the devil ?"

" No! I have not."

Then Justice Hathorne requested the afflicted children all to look at her, and see if this was the one that hurt them; and they all did look, and said she was one of them that did hurt them.

Then the children were all tormented, and Hathorne recommenced :

" Sarah Good, do you not see now what you have done? Why do you not tell the truth? Why do you thus torment these poor children ?"

" I do not torment them."

“Who do you employ, then?”

“I employ nobody; I scorn it.”

“How came they thus tormented, then?”

“What do I know? You bring others here, and now you charge me with it.”

“Why, who was it, then?”

“It might be some one you brought into the meeting-house with you.”

“We brought you into the meeting-house.”

“Yes; but you brought in two more.”

“Who was it, then, that tormented the children?”

“It might be Osburn.”

“What is it you say when you go muttering away from people’s houses?”

“If I must tell, I will tell.”

“Do tell us, then. What is it?”

“If I must tell, I will—it is the commandments. I may say them, I hope.”

“What commandment is it?”

“If I must tell you, I will tell—it is a psalm.”

“What psalm is it?”

After a long while she muttered part of a psalm.

“Who do you serve?”

"I serve God."

"What God do you serve?"

"The God that made heaven and earth."

As there was little to be gained by further examination of this prisoner, the constable was ordered to remove her, and Sarah Osburn was brought in and placed upon the stand.

This poor creature was, if any thing, more pitiable than the other. She had been a woman of respectable character, and of some standing in the community. Her first husband had died, leaving her a comfortable fortune, and two or more sons. She afterward married Osburn, who was much beneath her in social position. He had squandered her money, quarreled with her children, and deserted her; and she was sick in body and almost imbecile in mind.

Her examination was as follows:

"What evil spirit have you familiarity with?"

"Not any."

"Have you made no contract with the devil?"

"No; I never saw the devil in my life."

"Why do you hurt these children?"

"I do not hurt them."

"Who do you employ, then, to hurt them?"

"I employ nobody."

"What familiarity have you with Sarah Good?"

"None. I have not seen her for these two years."

"Where did you see her then?"

"One day, going to town."

"What communication had you with her?"

"I had only, 'How do you do?' or so. I do not know her by name."

"What did you call her then?"

Osburn made a stand at that, but at last she said she called her "Sarah."

"Sarah Good saith it was you that hurt the children."

"I do not know that the devil goes about in my likeness to do any hurt."

The foregoing shows the unfairness of the course taken by the court, and the evident intention to confuse the prisoners, and endeavor to entangle them into a contradiction in their answers.

Sarah Good had not intended to accuse Goody Osburn. She had only been led by the questions put to her to allow that Osburn might be guilty. The whole amount of what she had intended to say seems clearly this, that if the sufferings of the children, of the reality of which she did not seem to entertain a doubt, were caused by either Osburn or herself, it must be by Osburn, as she was conscious of her own entire innocence of it; and this, which was uttered only in self-defense, was cruelly perverted by the court into a positive accusation against her fellow-prisoner.

But to return to Sarah Osburn. Mr. Hathorne now desired all the children to stand up and look upon the prisoner, and see if they did not know her — which they did; and every one of them said she was one of them that did afflict them.

Three witnesses declared she had said that morning, "She was more like to be bewitched than that she was a witch;" and Mr. Hathorne asked her what made her say so.

She answered him she was frighted one time in her sleep, and either saw, or dreamed she saw, a thing like an Indian, all black, which did pinch her in her neck, and pulled her by the back of her head to the door of the house.

"And did you never see any thing else?" asked the examiner.

To which she replied, "No."

(Here it was said by some one in the meeting-house that she had said she would never believe that lying spirit any more.)

"What lying spirit is this? Hath the devil ever deceived you, and been false to you?"

"I do not know the devil. I never did see him."

"What lying spirit was it, then?"

"It was a voice that I thought I heard."

"And what did it propound to you?"

"That I should go no more to meeting. But I said I would go, and I did go next Sabbath-day."

"And were you never tempted any further?"

"No."

"Why did you yield thus far to the devil as never to go to meeting since?"

"Alas! I have been sick, and not able to go."

Here the examination of this prisoner, for the time, was ended, and she was removed. Certainly there seems to have been nothing elicited by this pointless questioning which could criminate the poor creature; and when we take into consideration the weakness of body and mind under which she was avowedly laboring, being half bed-ridden, and crazy, as her answers plainly show, she not being able to distinguish whether things she thought she saw and heard were dreams or realities, it would seem as if it must have been evident to any fair and impartial mind that, though her reason was clouded, her nature was essentially innocent and truthful.

The next one brought upon the stand was Tituba, the Indian slave-woman. As we have already said, this would seem to have been a stroke of policy. The fact of her having been one of their own number being calculated to disarm suspicion, while it is evident she had been in full council with the accusers, was under their control, and was well instructed as to all that she was to say and do.

To this end she begins, like the other two, by declaring her entire innocence, at which the children appear to be greatly tormented; but as she begins to *confess*, the children grow quiet, and she herself becomes afflicted before the eyes of the magistrates and the awe-stricken crowd, who looked on in blind belief and shuddering horror.

The object of all this was undoubtedly to show that the moment she confessed her sin, and repented of it, she had broken loose from her compact with the devil, and her power to afflict others had ceased at once; and the devil was wreaking his vengeance upon her through some other of his many confederates.

By her confession and repentance, she had passed from the condition of an *afflicter*, and had herself become one of the *afflicted* ones, and an accuser, naming Sarah Good, Sarah Osburn, and others as afflicting and tormenting herself and the children.

Her whole story is full of absurd and

monstrous fancies of devils, etc., and we will give some portions of her examination, as it serves to show the character of the woman, her intimate knowledge of all the children had said and done, and also showing by her own wild and unnatural images the impure source from which the pagan lore of the children was derived. The examination commenced exactly like the two others:

"Tituba, what evil spirit have you familiarity with?"

And, like the others, she answered, "None."

"Why do you hurt these children?"

"I do not hurt them."

"Who is it, then, that does?"

"The devil, for aught I know."

"Did you ever see the devil?"

"The devil came to me, and bid me serve him."

"Who have you seen?"

"Four women sometimes hurt the children."

"And who were they?"

"Goody Osburn and Sarah Good. I don't know who the others were. Sarah Good and Osburn would have me hurt the children, but I would not."

" When did you see them ?"

" Last night, at Boston."

" What did they say to you ?"

" They said, ' Hurt the children.' "

" And did you hurt them ?"

" No.   There is four women and one man —they hurt the children, and they lay it all upon me.   They tell me if I will not hurt the children, they will hurt me."

" But did you not hurt them ?"

" Yes ; but I will hurt them no more."

" Are you sorry that you did hurt them ?"
" Yes."

" And why, then, do you hurt them ?"

" They say, ' Hurt the children, or we will do worse to you.' "

" What have you seen ?"

" A man come to me, and say, ' Serve me.' "

" What service ?"

" Hurt the children.   Last night there was an appearance that said, ' Kill the children.'   And if I would not go on hurting the children, they would do worse to me."

" What is this appearance you see ?"

"Sometimes it is like a hog, and sometimes like a great dog."

"What did it say to you?"

"The black dog said, 'Serve me.' But I said, 'I am afraid.' He said if I did not, he would do worse to me."

"And what did you say to it?"

"'I will serve you no longer.' Then he said he would hurt me."

"What else have you seen?"

"Two cats — a red cat and a black cat."

"And what did they say to you?"

"They said, 'Serve me.'"

"When did you see them?"

"Last night. And they said, 'Serve me.' But I said I would not."

"What service?"

"Hurt the children."

"Did you not pinch Elizabeth Hubbard this morning?"

"The man brought her to me, and made me pinch her."

"Why did you go to Thomas Putnam's last night, and hurt his child?"

"They pull and haul me, and make me go."

"How did you go?"

"We ride upon sticks, and are there presently."

"Why did you not tell your master?"

"I was afraid. They said they would cut off my head if I told."

"Did you go through the trees, or over them?"

"We see nothing; but are there presently."

She also describes "a thing with a head like a woman, with two legs and wings;" and another "all hairy, but with only two legs, and going upright like a man."

But it is needless to continue these extracts any further. It seems strange, indeed, to us that at this senseless babble—which really appears too ridiculous to take pains to transcribe—grown men, of fair average common-sense and education, could ever have winced and shivered, and turned pale in shuddering horror as they listened; and yet it undoubtedly was so, for puerile and monstrous as it appears to us, it seems to have been fully conclusive to the mind of the learned court, for the prisoners were all three committed to jail to await further examinations.

These followed upon the second, third, fifth, and seventh of the month, when they were sent to Boston jail, where Sarah Osburn died in the following May. The child of Sarah Good, a little girl of five years of age, who had also been accused, died while in confinement.

As to the other two—Sarah Good and Tituba—as they will have no further connection with our story, we shall not return to them, and it may be as well to finish their histories here.

At one of the subsequent examinations of Sarah Good, one of the afflicted girls cried out that the prisoner, Good, had just stabbed her, and had broken the knife in so doing, in corroboration of which statement she produced a piece of a broken knife-blade. Upon which a young man then present produced the rest of the knife, which the court then examined, and declared to be the same. He then affirmed that he had broken the knife the day before, and had thrown away the piece, the accusing girl being present at the time. Upon which clear proof of her malicious mendacity, the court merely bade the sinful and falsified witness " to *tell them no more lies;*" and after this plain exposure of her guilt, she was still used as a witness against the unhappy prisoners.

It has also been recorded that at the execution of this Sarah Good, Mr. Noyes, the Salem minister—whose zeal certainly outran his discretion—followed the wretched woman even to the gallows, vehemently urging her to confess, and calling out to her, " You are a witch, and you know you are a witch." But "the trodden worm will turn at last," and, conscious of her own innocence of the dreadful crime, and maddened to desperation by his false and cruel accusations at such a moment, standing upon the very verge of that world where there is no respect of persons, the miserable creature cried out in frenzy from the steps of the ladder, " You are a liar ! I am no more of a witch than you are a wizard ; and, as you take away my innocent life, may God give you blood to drink !"

When, nearly twenty-four years after, Mr.

Noyes died of sudden and violent internal hemorrhage, bleeding profusely at the mouth, what wonder if it were long a commonly received tradition that the frantic words of the wronged and dying woman were thus fearfully verified?

The only record we find remaining of Tituba, the Indian woman, is that she afterward testified that her master did beat and otherwise abuse her, to make her confess, and accuse the others; and that what she had said in confessing and accusing others was in consequence of such usage from him; that he refused to pay her prison fees, and take her out of jail, unless she would stand to what she had said; and that consequently she remained in jail, until she was finally " sold for her fees."

If this is true, and there seems no reason to doubt it, it bears a fearful testimony against Mr. Parris, her master, as having been the unseen but moving power of this great tragedy.

The fearful delusion had now reached its height; its lamentable effects were widespread, and the whole country felt its horrors.   All business was interrupted or set aside, farm labors were neglected, cultivation was forgotten.   "It seemed," said the historian, "to strike an entire summer out of the year."

All contemplated improvements were given up ; farms and homesteads were sold out or abandoned ; and the terrified people, shocked at what had taken place, and still more in terror of what was yet to come—dreading where the bolt might strike next—hastened to quit the doomed neighborhood.

CHAPTER VIII.

ARCHITECTURAL DESIGNS.

"The earth no longer can afford
  Its old-time feuds and quarrels—
Hence! with the warrior's dented sword,
  The victor's blood-stained laurels!
The world has had enough of war,
  Of bloodshed and of clamor;
Honor to him who guides the saw,
  To him who wields the hammer."

GREAT, almost ineffably great, was the delight of old Winny when she first heard of the expected arrival of the feathered inmates. But if her delight could not find adequate expression, neither could it be wholly repressed.

"Wal, now, dat are is nice," she said, complacently. "Dat are is sum'pen like a present. Dat seems like as if we wuz folks— it makes a place look so much more respectabler-like to see dem sort o' critters round. I will say for't, hens are mighty 'spectable animals—'specially the roosters. An' den de eggs—why, goodness a massy! I tink eggs is allers the first fruits ob de season, I really do. I dun'no," she added, looking down reflectively, rubbing her arms alternately, and thoughtfully scraping up the sand where she stood with the broad side of her old, square-toed shoe—"I dun'no: a pig may be a more sociabler bird in his feelin's—I won't say dat he isn't. But den, yer see, he isn't so talkative-like, an' he isn't sich an easy boarder—he wants a deal more food, an' a deal more waitin' 'on, he does; an' he's a deal meaner-like too. A hen, now, she's kinder honest an' industr'us, an' free-hearted an' gen'rous—she pays her board as she goes along—an' egg mostly allers ebery day, an' now an' den, if she haz a chance, a brood of chickens. Wal, dat are is right; she couldn't do no better. But a pig—oh! he's a mighty fine gemmen to be waited 'on, an' he takes his ease like a gemmen, but he neber pays a cent on his board-bill as long as he libs —no, not till he dies; an' he wouldn't then if he could help hisself—not he, indeed! If he could have his will drawed up by a lawyer, I don't beliebe he'd leabe yer as much as a sassinger or a hasslet!—a mean thing —ha! I 'spize him! But, Alice, where will yer keep yer critters?"

"I don't just know, Winny. That is what I came out to ask you about. Don't you think we could contrive to make a hen-coop out of the farther end of the wood-shed? I mean if it were parted off. You don't make much use of that end of it, do you?"

"Not a bit ob use. I on'y keeps my soap-barr'l an' my ashes ober there; I kin fotch my soap ober this side jest as well as not, an' my ashes. Folks talks 'bout not wantin' to hab their ashes 'sturbed; law for me, I don't mind it a mite. 'Sturb 'um as much as yer like."

" Well, then, if we could get it parted off, wouldn't it make a nice hen-coop?"

" I should say it would be splenderous!"

" But, Winny, do you think grandmother will be willing?"

"I guess she won't be 'ginst nuffin' you want—she don't use to."

" That is true enough, Winny. She is very indulgent. The next thing is, how can we do it?"

"Wal, we must get boards, an' nail 'um up. Dar aint no udder way, as I knows on."

"Oh, yes; I know that. . But who shall we get to do it?"

Winny reflected a moment. "I dun'no; lem me see. Don't yer tink ole Drosky kin do it?"

"Drosky! I don't know. Who is Drosky, Winny?"

"Why, my ole dad."

"Your dad? What do you mean?—your father, Winny? Why, I never knew you had a father."

"Yer didn't now? Dat's queer. Why, I's had him eber an' eber so long. I had him when I warn't higher dan dat stool. Oh! longer; I's had him eber since I kin remember. I ruther tink I had him afore I war born. Lordy! I guess I's allers had him."

"Oh! I dare say. Only it seems strange I never heard of him before."

"Wal! really, it does now. He aint nuffin' to boast ob—Drosky aint. But I neber made no secret ob 'im. I aint 'shamed ob it; 'coz it's my misfortin', it aint my fault. I didn't buy 'im, nor beg 'im, nor steal 'im;

fact, I don't know jest how I did get 'im; I neber went a step out ob my way to pick 'im up. The Lord he sent him to me, I s'pose; an' I'm sure I wish he hadn't tort on't—I neber asked for no farders. I neber wanted none; an' I's sure sartin I'd be better off widout 'im."

"I don't know about that, Winny," said the laughing Alice. "But, Winny, what is he?"

"What is he? My farder? Why, an ole nigger, ob course. What else did yer tink he wuz? Look at me—do I look as though I 'longed to white folks?"

"No, no; you did not understand me, Winny. I meant what does he do for a living?"

"Bress us an' sabe us! he don't do no libin'. I haz to do de libin' for 'im; an' it's an awful sight o' libin' he takes too, I kin tell yer. Why, bress yer soul! dat are ole nigger, he'd eat a whole cabbidge an' a peck ob 'taters in a day, ebery day ob his black life, an' more too, if I'd let 'im. He aint got no conscience."

"But where does he live, Winny?"

"Oh! I's got a bunk for 'im out in de paster, an' he libs dar."

"But why did I never chance to see him before?   Why does he never come here?"

"Coz I won't let 'im.   Sez I to 'im, 'Drosky, yer ole sinner, look a here! if eber yer come a niggerin' roun' de house whar I libs, I'll sot de tidy-man at yer, I will.'   Oh! I tell yer, I haz to make 'im mind—he'd be awful imperdent if I didn't.   But I keeps 'im down; he's awful feared o' me.   If I jest clap hands and cry, 'Tidy-man! tidy-man! hist-st-st!' he'll run like rats."

"But, Winny, do you think he could build our hen-coop?"

"I 'clare I dun'no why not.   If a nigger can't build a hen-coop nor a pig-sty, what on arth kin he do?   You go an' ask leabe ob yer granny, an' if she says so, I'll go an' get ole dad, an' we'll see what he kin do."

Permission to build being readily obtained from Mrs. Campbell, Winny went out, and soon returned followed by her venerable parent; and of all the strange objects ever beheld in the shape of a man, old Drosky, take him all in all, was the most strange and singular.

He was evidently immensely old, and was

not more than four and a half feet high, and stooping at that. It seemed as if he had originally been a man of large frame, and, possibly, of proportionate height; but in the long course of his very protracted existence, every part of him that could shrink had shriveled up like a mummy, while the bony portions of his frame—his head, hands, feet, and joints—still retained their normal size, and looked, of course, unnaturally out of proportion.

The effect of the disproportionate size of his head was absurdly increased by an immense quantity of snow-white wool, which was pulled out at each side, till his head was as big as a peck measure. Beneath this snowy apex, his great black face, with its rolling, blinking eyes, was wonderfully effective. His body had been so bent by the weight of many years that it was nearly at right angles with his attenuated lower limbs, and yet his motions had all the sinewy spryness of a cat.

His dress was clean and whole—no, not whole, for its entirety consisted of patches of nearly every shade of black, blue, green, and brown, skillfully applied by Winny's frugal and industrious hands. If the too covetous sons of Jacob had been gifted, like their world-renowned brother, with prophetic dreams and visions, and, looking down the long roll of centuries, could have beheld old Drosky's many-hued garment, possibly the "coat of many colors" which their too partial old father gave to his favored darling would never have tempted them to envy, hate, and fratricide; the exodus into Egypt might never have taken place; and the world would have lost one of the sweetest and most pathetic of its Bible stories.

"Make yer manners, nigger! What yer tinkin' 'bout?" said Winny, authoritatively; and at once the old man began scraping his foot upon the ground, and butting with his woolly head like some vicious old ram, though evidently with more friendly intentions.

"Why, what a wonderfully old man! Why, Winny, how old is he?" said Alice, not knowing what to say.

"Oh, lors! I dun'no. Old?—he's old enuff for any ting, I guess. How old be yer, nigger—do yer know?"

"Te-hee! te-hee!" tittered the old man; "te-hee! te-hee! I dun'no, Winny, gal. I 'spect I's older dan you be; but I dun'no—te-hee! te-hee!"

"Wal, I shouldn't wonder if yer wuz," said Winny, quietly regarding him.

"And have you got a mother too, Winny?" inquired Alice.

"A mudder?—no, I guess not. I neber heerd o' none. Say, ole nigger!" turning to her father, "we aint got no mudder, hab we?"

"Te-hee! te-hee! No, no, Winny, gal," tittered the old man. "No mudder! no mudder! no, no!—te-hee! te-hee!"

"I tort not," said Winny, turning to Alice. "Yer see we two haz been pardners a many years, an' I guess dar aint no mudder in de biz'ness; I neber see none roun'. Yer didn't neber hab no mudders, did ye, Drosky?"

"Te-hee! te-hee! Neber a mudder, gal—never; te-hee! te-hee!"

"Is he so very deaf, Winny?" asked Alice, finding that Winny raised her voice almost to a scream whenever she addressed her father.

"Deaf?—he? No, nor blind nuther. I wish he wuz; at his time o' life it wud be a sight more respectabler-like if he wuz one or t'other o' 'um. He ought to be 'shamed o' hisself, not to have no infarmities, an' he so awful ole. It 'pears as if the Lord had clean forgot the ole fellow—don't it now? An' 'tween you an' I, Alice, I rather 'spect he haz."

"Oh, Winny, don't talk so," said Alice; her own tender, filial feelings toward her only relative, her grandmother, making Winny's unfilial disrespect to her aged parent seem shocking to her—"Oh! don't talk so; you would be so sorry if he were to die."

"Die! Who die? He?—dad? Cotch 'im at it; I'd like to see 'im do it. Not he! He aint a goin' to die, I know. He don't want to, an' he dun'no how to, if he did. He neber died in all his life, an' I guess he aint a goin' to larn now. He's too old to larn nuffin'. He'll neber die; he wouldn't know how to begin."

"But, Winny," said Alice, returning to the main point in question, "do you think he can do what we want?"

"I don't see why he can't; for the massy's soul's sake, why not? But I'll ax him. Here, you ole rogue ob a sinner," she said, addressing her parent, "you kin build a hen-coop—you, can't yer?"

"Te-hee! te-hee! No, Winny, gal—no!" tittered the cracked old voice; "I can't make no hen-coop—te-hee!"

"Yer can't? An' why not can't yer? Yes, yer can, too. Why can't yer?"

"Te-hee! te-hee! Winny, gal, aint got no boards—can't make hen-coop widout boards —te-hee! te-hee!"

"Lordy! yer ole fool! we wuz 'spectin' to fin' yer de boards—course we wuz. Did yer tink we 'spected yer to make it out ob yer own ole skin? An' if yer had de boards, nigger, kin yer build it den? Come, now, be smart—kin yer make it den, say?"

"Te-hee! te-hee! No, Winny, gal!—no, no!"

"Why not? Yes, yer *could.* Why not?"

"'Coz it takes nails, Winny—nails, gal! Te-hee! te-hee!"

"Yer darned ole fool! An' if yer had boards an' nails — whatever else wud yer want?"

"Te-hee! te-hee! Winny, ole gal, hammer an' saw—hammer an' saw—te-hee! te-
hee!"

"Lord sake, yes! Yer'd want hammer
an' saw—ob course yer wud; but if yer had
dem, kin yer do it?"

"Te-hee! te-hee! Winny, yes—yes, I kin,
I kin. I'll make hen-coop fas' enuff."

"Werry well, den; I'll fin' yer all dem
tings. Take off yer jacket, ole man, an' 'rouse
dat are ole barr'l ob soap ober dis way, an'
put it here. Do yer see, nigger?—put it
here."

Certainly the old man's strength had not
diminished with his size. He moved the
barrel with the greatest apparent ease, and
placed it according to orders, and then shov-
eled away the ashes from the proposed site
of the new partition; and by the time these
two jobs were completed, Winny had mus-
tered the necessary boards, nails, hammer, and
saw. It was amusing to Alice to see the
professional earnestness of the old man, as
he bent the saw in his withered hands to
test its temper, and tried its teeth upon his
own broad thumb; and, there being no fault

to be found in this important auxiliary, he was satisfied, and the work was begun in earnest.

A fair division of labor is one of the useful discoveries of modern times; but if our friends had never heard of it as a principle, they certainly availed themselves of it as a fact. First, Alice, as the owner, founder, and projector, pondered and considered and decided what she wished to have done. She represented the *theoretic* element. Next, the more experienced matron, Mrs. Campbell, took her grandchild's crude imaginings into wise consideration, and decided how it was to be done. She was clearly the *practical* member. Next came Winny, who held the highest *executive* power; she took her directions from her mistress, measured and marked and adjusted the boards in their places, and showed her father how to do it. And last of all came in old Drosky, the *mechanical* power, who did the hammering and sawing —or, as Winny pithily phrased it, " she druv old dad, an' dad druv the nails."

At all events, they worked well together, and made a very harmonious quartette, and the work went gayly on. It is just possible that there may have been more noise and clatter when the Tower of Babel was run up. But then that was a more imposing structure, there were more people engaged in it, and it was in the Old World; but this was pretty well for a new country—three women, an old man, and a hen-coop—and made some noise in the world.

When the work was about half finished, Alice, who, owning not a penny of her own in the wide world, was, of course, of a very liberal and generous disposition—as penniless people usually are—proposed that old Drosky should stop and rest, and have something to eat, observing to Winny that she was sure he must be tired, and hungry too.

"No, he aint—not a bit ob it," said Winny, with a reproving and admonitory wink of her eye, and a shake of her sagacious old head at Alice. "He aint a mite hungry yet, yer know," and as she spoke she looked full in old Drosky's face, whose hungry eyes spoke a very different language. "You aint not a mite hungry now, nigger; but I 'spects yer will be when yer work is done, and den I 'clare I guess yer'll get sum'pen to eat—I do."

"Shoo!" she said, sotto-voce, turning to Alice, "yer don' know dat are ole man as well as I do—he's a mighty powerful han' to eat. Yer sot 'im at it now, an' I guess yer cocks an' hens will hev to stan' roun' all night for want ob a roost to sot down on. Keep 'im at it till de work's done, I tell yer, an' den stan' clear — an' you'll see!" and Drosky resumed his work submissively but regretfully. But at length the work was completed—the partition was all up; the broken hinge of the door was replaced; slats were put over the window, to allow air, but not egress; the waste ashes were spread over the floor, "to keep off wermin," as Winny explained to Alice; a clothes-pole was put up for a roost; and two old boxes, filled with hay, were introduced to offer suggestive ideas to any well-disposed hen who might be thriftily inclined to pay for her board in eggs and chickens; and all was declared in readiness for the expected tenants.

Alice was delighted—but still more charm-

ed was old Drosky. He went in, and silently contemplated the little apartment with
intense satisfaction; possibly he was admiring
the work of his own hands—more probably
he was thinking how superior the accommo-
dations were to his own; but he stayed so
long in wrapt contemplation that Winny
had to interfere at last.

"I 'clare for't," she said, "I b'liebe dat ole
nigger ob mine wud jest stay an' sot in dar
all night, if we'd let 'im; pity he could'nt
sot for yer hens, Alice—'twould save dere
time, an' it's jest 'bout what he's fit for."
But Winny knew of a potent charm sufficient to draw him out.

"Kim a he'ar, nigger, an' get sum'pen to
eat;" and the old man was at her heels in a
moment.

Laughingly Alice followed them to a table,
which Winny had improvised out of two
barrels and a board for his express use.
Here the indulgent daughter laid out two
or three dozen of cold boiled potatoes; half
a peck of cold baked beans, with a corresponding lump of pork; half of a pie; a loaf
of bread; a huge bit of cheese; a ham-bone;

a saucerful of pickles; a bowl of tea; and a can of cider.

With laughing eyes, full of mingled mirth and amazement, Alice stood quietly by and watched the old darkie make his way through this heterogeneous mass of food, with the celerity and the apparent ease with which an able mower cuts his swath through a field of ripened grain; keeping up all the time an incessant shuffling of his feet, as if that were some part of the machinery by which he was able to accomplish so much in so short a time; but when, after making a clean sweep over the board, he turned his wishful eyes upon Winny with an Oliver Twistical expression, Alice could not help laughing. "He doesn't mean that he wants more, does he, Winny?"

"Oh, no; laws bress us, no; he tinks he does; but he dun'no. No, no, nigger! yer won't get nuffin' more here — yer kin go home now an' hav' yer supper."

But when Alice, furnished with the money by her grandmother, was about to offer it to old Drosky, the dusky hand of Winny was interposed. "Hi! hi! Alice; don't yer go to giv' it to 'im—yer giv' it to me; he don't know nuffin' about money — I'll take it. Here, nigger! here's some coppers for yer to buy 'bacca wid; an' now make yer manners an' take yerself off—do yer hear?"

Again, in obedience to his daughter, the ram-like butting and scraping performance was gone through with, and Drosky moved off; but at the gate he paused, looked back with admiring eyes at the work of his hands, and half turned, as if to enter the coop again; but his daughter's eye was upon him; a sudden clapping of hands, a loud shout—"Hist! hist! Drosky! *tidy-man! tidy-man!*"—and poor old Drosky was off like a shot, just as the cart drove up with Goody Nurse's present.

With great cackling and squalling, laughing and talking, the new-comers were released from their confinement and introduced to their new quarters, where they went to roost at once, as if the events of the day and their unexpected journey had been almost too much for them, and they knew that "what was new at night would still be new in the morning."

Alice looked in upon them with much pleasure as they crowded close together, side by side, on the low roost, and shut and buttoned the door upon them with a proud feeling of ownership, as novel to her as it was delightful.

CHAPTER IX.

GOODY REBECCA NURSE.

"Daring to shake, with rude, irreverent hands,
From Life's frail glass the last slow-ebbing sands."

AMONG the best known, most influential, and widely respected of all the families of Salem village was the large family of Francis Nurse.

"Goodman," or "Grandfather," or "Landlord Nurse," which were the several titles of respect usually accorded to him, as the honored head and patriarch of his numerous family of children and grandchildren, was then about seventy-six years of age.

He appears to have been a man of great and acknowledged respectability; a person of much energy and stability of character, and his judgment was much relied upon by his neighbors; he being frequently appointed to act the part of umpire in disputes, arbitrator on conflicting claims, and also as committee-man and juror. Goodman Nurse had been a mechanic in Salem, but having by patient industry accumulated a little money, he removed to Salem village, where, in the year 1650, he purchased the great "Townsend Bishop Farm," as it was termed, a tract of about three hundred acres of land, much of it already improved, at the cost of £400. He was at this time a fine, hearty, hale, and vigorous old man; his wife, Rebecca Nurse, was about one year younger than himself.

She was an eminently Christian woman, full of good works; a regular member of long standing in the mother church at Salem; but after their removal to Salem village, by reason of her advanced age and consequent frequent infirmities, often a worshiper at the nearer church in the village, although never formally united with them. Goody Nurse seems to have been one of those rarely gifted women who unite the solid worth and excellence of a deeply religious character with the lighter graces of a cheerful and attractive manner; kind-hearted, single-minded, and free-spoken.

This worthy couple had brought up a large and exemplary family of children. They had four sons—Samuel, John, Francis, and Benjamin; and four daughters—Rebecca, married to Thomas Preston; Mary, the wife of John Tarbell; Elizabeth, the wife of William Russel; and Sarah, then unmarried, but afterward the wife of Michael Bowdon, of Marblehead.

Francis Nurse, senior, having by the united industry of himself and his children cleared off all the encumbrances upon his large estate, had apportioned it among his several children, reserving a homestead for himself; and his son Samuel, and his two sons-in-law, Thomas Preston and John Tarbell, had already established themselves there near their parents, having separate households and gardens upon the land thus conveyed to them by their father; and a happier, more united, or more respectable family can hardly be imagined than were the Nurses at the time the great delusion of witchcraft first broke out.

Thomas Preston, one of the sons-in-law, was

at first a believer in the sufferings of the " afflicted children;" but many others of the
family circle, and among them the beloved
and venerable mother, refused credence to
their pretensions, and had absented themselves from attendance at the village church
in consequence of the great and scandalous
disturbances which they created there.

It is also noticeable that the Nurse family
had been opposed to the party or faction who
had been so zealous in favor of Mr. Bayley,
the former minister, and they had thus drawn
upon themselves the ill-will of Mrs. Ann Putnam, who had been one of his most zealous
partisans, and was now one of the most fanatical of the accusers.

Mrs. Nurse, who was a free-spoken, active
body, had taken a decided part in these
church discussions : it is singular to note how
in all parish difficulties the female portion
are the most zealous, the most belligerent, and
the most vituperative. No doubt Mrs. Nurse
had been free in the expression of her senti-
ments upon both these subjects—it was the
nature of the woman to be so ; and unfriendly
remarks about the children, any doubt of the

truth of their statements or the reality of their sufferings, were sure to be carried to them at once, and of course suggested to them new victims to accuse as the authors of all their sufferings and torments.

There had been for some time a half-concealed intimation that some one more noted than any of the previous victims was to be brought to justice, and expectation and fear were at their highest, when at length it was stealthily whispered about that Goodwife Nurse was suspected and was to be cried out upon.

At first, of course, the rumor was indignantly discredited; the quiet, unobtrusive virtues of the aged, Christian, village matron, her well-known charities and kindliness of heart setting defiance to the monstrous charge against her.

But day by day the rumor grew that she was to be called out, and at last two of her personal friends, Israel Porter and his wife Elizabeth, were requested to go to the Farm, see Mrs. Nurse, and tell her that several of the afflicted ones had accused her.

As the persons thus selected and sent were

her friends, it would seem to intimate that the painful visit they were to make was undertaken in a friendly spirit, and was intended to warn the unsuspecting woman of the peril in which she stood, and very possibly they may have hoped that she would take the alarm and save herself by flight.

Entering the grounds, now all bright and smiling in the new promise of their spring beauty, the anxious friends reached the house, which was then regarded as a spacious and elegant one; it had once been the abode of some of the choicest and best spirits in New England — here Bishop had spent his wealth to beautify the spot, and here he and Chickering and Ingersoll had exercised the rites of liberal and elegant hospitality; and now it was the happy home of an honest and prosperous family.

Entering, they found the venerable and unsuspecting hostess in her usual place. She welcomed them gladly, with all her wonted friendly hospitality; although, as she told them in answer to their inquiry, in a rather weak and low condition, having been sick and confined to the house for nearly a week.

Then they asked how it was with her otherwise. To which the patient, cheerful-hearted old Christian replied, "that she blessed God for it, that she had had more of his presence in this sickness than at some other times, but not so much as she desired; but she would, with the apostle, 'press forward to the mark,'" with other passages from Scripture to the like purpose. This was not the cant of a hypocritical piety—it was the common mode of expression among Christian believers in those times; and it seemed as if her religious beliefs and the natural buoyancy of her spirits kept her up under the weight of her years and infirmities.

After a little conversation relative to personal and domestic matters, such as is usual among friendly neighbors, she naturally and of her own accord alluded to the great affliction which had broken out among them, and which was of course the most common subject of conversation.

She spoke very kindly of Mr. Parris's family, and said she was much grieved for them, but she had not been to see them because she had once been subject to fits herself, and she did not wish to see them, as people told her their sufferings were awful to witness; that she pitied them with all her heart, and had prayed to God for them; but she had heard that there were some persons accused whom she fully believed were as innocent as she was herself.

After a little more conversation of this sort, the visitors told her that they had heard a report that she too had been spoken against.

"Well," she said, "if it be so, the will of the Lord be done."

Then for a while she sat perfectly still, as if utterly amazed at what she had heard—and well she might be. The mind of the aged and saintly woman could not admit the fact; it was all too unnatural— too monstrous—that her good name could be thus vilely traduced.

How could she for a moment believe that her own neighbors, whom she had loved and befriended—that the members of the church where she had worshiped—would listen to such a horrible accusation.

After a little silent reflection, and doubtless an inward prayer, the poor woman said, sadly, "Well, as to this thing, I am as innocent as the child unborn. But surely," she added, "what sin hath God found out in me, unrepented of, that he should lay such a heavy affliction upon me in my old age?"

The pious and loving old woman, the mother, grandmother, and great-grandmother of a large and affectionate family, made no attempt to escape or evade her enemies, as she might possibly even then have done; but fully conscious of her own integrity, and with a heart full of love and good-will to others, she felt sure her friends, her townspeople, and her fellow-worshipers would justify and defend her.

But her inexorable fate was hurrying along; and on the 23d of March a warrant was duly issued against her on the complaint of Edward and Jonathan Putnam; and on the next morning, at eight o'clock, she was arrested — torn, sick and feeble as she was, from the clinging arms of her weeping daughters and indignant husband and sons, and brought up for examination by the marshal, George Herrick.

At this time, it would seem that, though many accusations had been made, and several, after undergoing a preliminary examination, had been committed, there had been no actual trials, and, of course, no convictions or condemnations; consequently it may be that the prisoner and her friends, although fully alive to the disgrace and obloquy of such a charge, did not realize the awful peril of death in which she was now standing.

It was bitterness enough that, sick and feeble as she was in health, infirm and aged, she was taken all unprepared from her quiet and comfortable home, and the tender care of her devoted husband and children, upon a charge so utterly unfounded, and subjected to an examination so harrowing and so disgraceful.

The preliminary examination of this venerable "Mother in Israel" took place at once in the village meeting-house, the magistrate Hathorne commencing the proceedings, making himself the mouthpiece of the assembly; and it is noticeable all through these examinations that Hathorne, full of zeal, took an active and prominent part in them, almost assuming the office of prosecuting officer, while his brother magistrate, Justice Corwin, although present, and signing the commitments, seems to have been a silent, passive, and almost unwilling agent in the affair; so evidently was this the case, that his lukewarmness excited the displeasure of the accusing girls, and they made several attempts to cry out against members of his family.

Hathorne began in this case by addressing one of the afflicted ones:

"What do you say? Have you seen this woman hurt you?"

"Yes, she beat me this morning."

"Abigail, have you been hurt by this woman?"

"Yes, I have."

Here Ann Putnam had a terrible fit, and cried out that it was Rebecca Nurse who was afflicting her. When Ann's fit was over, and order restored in court, Hathorne continued:

"Goody Nurse, here are two who complain of you as hurting them; what do you say to it?"

"I can say, before my Eternal Father, I am innocent; and God will clear my innocency."

Hathorne was apparently touched for the time by her language and bearing, and said to her:

"Here is never a one in the assembly but desires it; but if you be guilty, pray God discover you."

The prisoner again affirmed her innocence, asserting in answer to the charge of hurting any one, that she had been sick, and not out of doors for some days.

This simple statement seemed to awaken a doubt of her being guilty in the mind of the magistrate, and the popular feeling seemed turning in her favor, when the wife of Thomas Putnam—who had an old grudge against her on account of her opposition to Mr. Bayley, and whose wild, passionate excitement carried her beyond the control of her reason—suddenly cried out with a loud voice:

"Did you not bring the black man with you? Did you not bid me tempt God and die? How often have you eat and drank your own damnation?"

This sudden and terrible charge, uttered with frantic cries and vehement gesticulations, roused the listening multitude to horror. Even the prisoner herself seemed to be shocked at the woman's evident madness, and, raising her hands to heaven, she fervently ejaculated—"Oh, Lord! help me, help me!"

Upon this all the afflicted children were tormented; and when all this various tumult had subsided, Hathorne again addressed the prisoner:

"Do you not see what a solemn condition these are in, that when your hands are loosed they are afflicted?"

Then Mary Walcott and Elizabeth Hubbard accused her, but she answered:

"The Lord knows I have not hurt them; I am an innocent person."

Then Hathorne continued:

"It is very awful to see all these agonies; and you, an old professor, thus charged with contracting with the devil by the effects of it; and yet to see you stand with dry eyes, when there are so many wet."

It was considered one proof of a witch

that she could not shed tears, and to this she said, "You do not know my heart."

Hathorne continued: "You would do well, if you are guilty, to confess, and give glory to God."

"I am innocent," she replied, "as the child unborn."

Then he told her that they charged her with having familiar spirits come to her bodily person then and there, and asked her:

"Now, what do you say to that?"

"I have none, sir."

"If you have, confess, and give glory to God. I pray God clear you if you be innocent, and if you are guilty, discover you; and therefore give me an upright answer: Have you any familiarity with these spirits?"

"No, I have none; but with God alone."

At this point it seems as if the magistrate began to waver as to her guilt; after questioning her upon many other things, he seems almost convinced of her innocence.

"You do know," he said, "whether you are guilty, and have familiarity with the devil; these testify that there is a black man whispering in your ear, and birds about you; what do you say to it?"

"That it is all false; I am clear."

"Possibly you may apprehend you are no witch; but have you not been led aside by temptations in that way?"

"No, I have not."

"Have you not had visible appearances, more than what is common in nature?"

"I have none; nor ever had in my life."

"Do you think these suffer voluntarily or involuntarily?"

"I can not tell."

"That is strange; every one can judge."

"I must be silent."

"They accuse you of hurting them, and you think it is not unwillingly, but by design; you must then look upon them as murderers."

"I can not tell what to think of it."

This last answer was considered as equivalent to calling them murderers; but this she denied, saying that being a little hard of hearing she did not quite understand the question, and had meant only to say that she could not tell what to make of their conduct.

"Do you think that these suffer against their wills, or not?"

"I do not think they suffer against their wills."

"But why did you never go to see these afflicted persons?"

"Because I was afraid I should have fits too."

Upon every motion of the prisoner's body the children had fits, upon which Hathorne said:

"Is it not an unaccountable thing that when you are examined these persons are afflicted?"

Seeing that he and all the others believed in her accusers, her only reply to this was:

"I have nobody to look to—but God."

As she said this she naturally attempted to raise her hands, upon which the afflicted ones were taken with great fits.

When order was again restored after all this tumult, the examiner continued:

"Do you believe these afflicted persons are bewitched?"

"I do think they are."

Goody Nurse was a clear-minded but un-

educated woman; she held the common opinion of her times—she believed in witchcraft,
and was willing to allow that the children
were bewitched; but she knew her own innocence, and she only asserted that and said,
"Would you have me belie myself?"

At length—being old, sick, and feeble,
worn out both in mind and body, and wearied with all she had thus undergone in this
long examination—the poor woman's head
drooped in very weakness; and at once, to
the consternation of the court and spectators, the necks of all the children were bent
in the same way.

Elizabeth Hubbard's neck appeared fixed,
and could not be moved, and Abigail Williams cried out:

"Set up Goody Nurse's head, or the maid's
neck will be broke;" whereupon some one
holding up the prisoner's head, the neck of
the other was righted at once.

Then the Rev. Mr. Parris read aloud a
declaration of what Thomas Putnam's wife
had said while in her fits—that the apparition of Goody Nurse had come to her at several times, and had horribly tortured her;
and then Hathorne asked her:

" What do you think of this ?"

" I can not help it; the devil may appear in my shape."

At the close of this long and most one-sided examination, where all the power and subtlety were with the examiner, and the unfortunate prisoner stood alone and unsupported, she was committed to Salem jail to await further examination; and there, doubtless, in common with all the others committed on the same charge, she was put in chains.

All this time the prevailing excitement was artfully heightened and kept up by lectures and sermons by Mr. Parris and Mr. Lawson, in which, by ingenious and laborious research of both the Old and New Testament histories, they proved and enlarged upon the nature and evidences of witchcraft.

After the lapse of a week preparations were made to renew operations, and to attempt to give to them a new and more commanding character; and, as new complaints were constantly being made, new arrests were issued, and the marshal received orders to bring his prisoners into the meeting-house in Salem on April eleventh.

This was not to be an examination before the two local magistrates, as the others had been, but before the highest legal tribunal in the colony—the Honorable Thomas Danforth, deputy governor, and his council being present.

But we do not propose to give the details of these trials; it is enough to say that the consummate tact and boldness of the accusing girls deluded every body.

No necromancers have ever surpassed them in sleight-of-hand and simulation. It has been said that in their strange performances, in which they had now perfected themselves by long practice, they equaled the ancient sorcerers and magicians. Of their fearful blasphemies, the horrible inventions, the monstrous fancies of the devil-worship, the fiendish sacraments, and other revolting ritual of which they accused their victims, we can only say that, while it was fully calculated to produce an overwhelming effect upon minds so imbued with a belief in all the superstitions of those days, they are to us, in our more enlightened age, simply too tedious and revolting to be transcribed upon our pages; and while we wonder at the marvelous dexterity of the girls in their performances, the principal interest for us is derived from the evidence they give, that all this fearful imagery was beyond the invention of youthful minds, and reveal the fact that some older and more experienced hand was moving unseen behind them.

At the close of this examination, Mrs. Nurse and five others were fully committed for trial, and were sent to Boston jail for safe keeping.

The court met again June 29th, and Mrs. Nurse was put upon trial; but the character of the venerable old woman was too well known not to have created many friends; time had given rise to reflection, and many persons, who had believed in other cases, paused, and hesitated to believe her guilty; and many, who had been silent through fear, now came forward boldly in her defense. Testimonials of her moral worth and unblemished character were got up and signed by persons of the highest respectability, and among these names appears that of Jonathan Putnam, one of the very men who had procured the warrant against her.

So deeply were the jurors impressed with the proofs of the virtue and Christian excellence of her character, that, in spite of the clamors of the spectators, the monstrous charges brought against her by the accusers, and even the plain leaning of the court against her, they brought in their verdict of "Not guilty."

But immediately all the accusers in court, and shortly after all the afflicted out of the court, made a great and hideous outcry, to the amazement not only of the many spectators, but of the court itself.

One of the judges expressed himself as not being fully satisfied; another of them said that they would have her indicted anew; and the chief justice intimated to the jury that they had not well considered one expression used by the prisoner.

This induced the jury to ask leave to go out again, and reconsider their verdict.

The point in question was this, that when one of the accused, who had confessed to being a witch (as several of the poor creatures were induced to do, in hope of thus making their escape from death), was brought up as a witness against her, Goody Nurse had said, "Why do you bring her? *She is one of us.*"

The foreman of the jury afterward stated that, upon considering this point, he could not tell what to make of her words—"she is one of us;" that he had returned to the court and stated his doubts; and that the prisoner, being still at the bar, she gave no reply or explanation, which made the words seem strong evidence against her (as if by them she acknowledged that she was one of the avowed witches).

The foreman having thus stated the case, and receiving no reply or explanation of the words from the prisoner, returned to the jury, who thereupon reconsidered their vote, and brought in a second verdict of "Guilty," upon which she was condemned, and sentenced to be hanged upon the coming 19th of July.

When the prisoner was afterward informed of this question, she explained her meaning to have been simply this, that the witness in question, being herself one of the prisoners, she did not think her evidence ought to be taken against her fellow-prisoners; but that being hard of hearing, and also full of grief and terror, she did not understand the meaning given to her words; and no one informing her how the matter stood, she had no chance to explain. Even after her condemnation, the governor saw cause to grant her a reprieve; but the accusers made such an outcry that he was induced to recall it.

"In a capital case," says the careful historian from whom we have gathered some of these facts, "the court often refuses the verdict of 'guilty,' but rarely sends a jury out to reconsider one of 'not guilty.'"

CHAPTER X.

EXCOMMUNICATION.

"None shall weep for thee—none shall pray for thee;
  Never a parting psalm be sung;
Never a priest shall point death's way for thee,
  Never a passing bell be rung."

FTER the fearful sentence had been pronounced, Mrs. Nurse was again taken to Salem jail, and there kept, loaded with chains and bound with cords, until her execution, it seeming to be the general belief that more restraint was needed for witches than for any other criminals.

But a new affliction was preparing for the aged and suffering Christian.

Upon the 3d of July, in the morning of the Sabbath-day, at the close of the services, after the sacrament of the Lord's Supper had been administered, it was propounded by the elders, and unanimously consented to by the Church members (by those who had just been commemorating the love of Him who died for sinners), that Sister Rebecca Nurse being a convicted witch, and by sentence of the court condemned to die, she should be excommunicated by the Church; and this was accordingly done on the afternoon of the same day.

Can the imagination picture any thing more revolting to all good feeling? At the very time when she stood most in need of the prayers and support of her Christian friends and fellow-worshipers, she was to be ruthlessly struck out of their communion, denied their sympathy, and cast off, reviled, and contemned by those in whose devotions she had so often taken a part.

Of course, this intended ceremonial was widely made known. The great meeting-house in Salem was crowded to its utmost capacity, in every nook and corner; the two ministers, or "ruling elders," as they were then termed, Mr. Higginson and Mr. Noyes, were both in the pulpit; the deacons and other elders all in their places, when the sheriff and the constables brought in their prisoner, heavily manacled and bound with cords, and placed her in the broad aisle.

Then the Rev. Mr. Noyes, rising like an accusing spirit, pronounced upon her the stern and awful sentence of the Church, which was then regarded as not only excluding her from the Church on earth, but as closing against her the very gates of heaven. Believing she had already transferred her allegiance to the devil, he then and there formally made her over, body and soul, to the great enemy forever and ever.

How the noble but grief-stricken old woman met this new and most appalling stroke of refined cruelty, neither history nor tradition has told us—but it were needless. Our own hearts can reproduce the terrible picture. We can almost see her aged form, as with slow and fettered steps she passed up the accustomed aisle, with the stern guardians of the law on either side of her, the hushed and awe-smitten crowd shrinking away from the pollution of her touch.

We can see the dim, sad eyes turning their piteous gaze from side to side, hoping to catch one glance of love or sympathy or pity. In vain. If pity or sympathy were there, only the bowed head and averted face manifested it.   In that dark hour, like her Master, "the Man of sorrows," she stood forsaken and alone.   We can see the quivering of her whole frame, as the stern, terrible words fall upon her clouded hearing, and see her waver and shrink and totter, as if the summer thunder-bolt had blasted her. It is but for a moment: the weak woman has faltered--but the believing disciple stands firm again; she knows in whom she has believed—she knows that her "Redeemer liveth;" and trusting in his love and power, she, who has meekly followed his example through life, follows it even now.   We see her fold her fettered arms across her submissive breast, as, raising her dim eyes to heaven, she faintly murmurs, in his own words, "Father, forgive them; for they know not what they do."

When this mockery of religion on the part of the Church was over, she was again taken to Salem jail, where she remained until the 19th of July, when she was hung at Gallow's Hill.

There seem to be two distinct sources from which we are permitted to see a beautiful and softening light thrown over the tragical horrors of this dark picture of fanatical persecution. The one is the calm, unwavering constancy, and the unbending fortitude of the sufferer herself—aged even beyond the allotted "threescore years and ten," infirm of health, suffering still from the effects of a recent illness and her long and rigorous confinement—no persecution could break down her trust in God, or her assurance of her own innocence and integrity of heart.

She was urged by her enemies to confess her guilt, and she well knew that only by confession could she hope to save herself from the horrors of an impending and ignominious death; but she repelled them with scorn: "Would you have me belie myself?" and their threats had no power to move her.

No doubt some of her family or friends, seeing her thus in mortal peril, may, in their loving earnestness, have importuned her to the same course; but, if so, she was proof against their affectionate pleadings. Life was pleasant to her, indeed—home and its loving endearments had never seemed so sweet; but more precious still was the immortal soul, which put its faith in God, and knew its own integrity. What to her were her few remaining days of the life on earth, that she should barter for them the blessed hopes of the life eternal?—and she stood firm.

The other beautiful and mitigating circumstance is the deep love and unwavering trust of her husband and children. They never doubted or forsook her. Day after day, early and late, braving the scoffs of the jeering and reviling crowd, they were at the prison, cheering her by the assurance of their unshaken love and trust, and supporting her by their tender ministrations. They left no means unessayed for her vindication: they put in new evidence; they got up petitions, testimonials, and remonstrances; they walked beside her to the place of execution, cheering and sustaining her to the last by the assurances of their unabated and devoted love; and when all was over, at the risk of

their own lives, they obtained the dishonor-
ed but beloved remains, and privately and
by night gave them tender and reverent burial in their own land, where they rest to
this day at peace among her kindred.

CHAPTER XI.

THE MERCHANT'S WIFE.

"I call her *angel*—but *he* called her wife."

IT was in Salem, at noon, on Saturday, and the court, which held its sessions in the great First Church on Essex Street, had just risen and adjourned to the coming week, when Justice Jonathan Corwin, leaving the heated and oppressive air of the court-room (oppressive at once to mind and body), passed with slow, dignified steps, thoughtfully depressed head, and arms crossed behind him, down Essex Street, to a large house then standing upon the site of the present market-place in Derby Square, and occupied by the Honorable Colonel William Browne.

Entering unannounced, with the familiar air of a frequent and ever welcome guest, he passed through the hall which divided the house, and opening the glass doors which closed it at its lower extremity, came out upon a vine-shaded porch or veranda, which ran across a portion of the southern or back part of the house. Below the wide, easy steps spread the flower-garden, now bright in all the radiance of its summer hues; and at the extremity of the little flowery domain, the quiet, blue waters of " Browne's Cove " were rippling and flashing in the sunny light.

Upon a straight, high-backed chair in this cool and shady seclusion sat his sister, Mrs. Browne, the mistress of the establishment, still a fair and graceful matron, although now past the earlier bloom and freshness of her youthful beauty.

She was richly and becomingly dressed, after the rather gorgeous fashion of the day. A loosely fitting negligee of rich satin, of that peculiar shade of lilac-pink which we so often see in Copley's matchless portraits, was worn over a pale sea-green petticoat of quilted silk, and fell in sheeny folds to the ground. The dress was cut low and open in front, leaving her neck partially bare, and so were her white arms to the elbow; but both neck and arms were shaded and relieved by wide ruffles of the costliest lace. Her soft and still abundant dark hair was drawn off from her brow, and combed over a crape cushion—much as modern taste dictates to its votaries of the present day—and being gathered into a clasp or band at the back of the head, the ends were suffered to flow in loose, waving curls over her neck and shoulders. A string of large pearls, clasped closely around her slender throat, and a brilliant pin at the knot of ribbons at the top of her bodice (or stomacher, as it was termed), connected by a glittering chain to the massive gold watch and equipage at her side, were the common ornaments which marked her rank in life, at a period when female domestics were not accustomed to outshine their mistresses in extravagance of dress and demeanor.

We have said that she was no longer in extreme youth, but the fair face was still smooth and delicately tinted; and time, which had added thoughtfulness to the open brow, and penetration to the deep, darkly lustrous eyes, smiling beneath their finely arched brows, had left unimpaired the almost child-like tenderness of the sweet lips.

"Good-morning, Sister Browne," said the brother, stepping out upon the veranda, and bending over her with the stately courtesy of the times, he pressed a light kiss upon her fair, round cheek.

"Good-morning, Jonathan," responded the matron, offering her hand in hospitable greet-ing.

"Husband not come home yet, Hannah?" inquired the visitor.

"Not yet," she replied. "The colonel is later than usual very often nowadays. They are about fitting out two of their vessels, and my husband is often detained at the store quite beyond the usual hour. The times are so out of joint at present that it is almost impossible to procure the necessary labor. Every body seems to be taken out of themselves, and all work is neglected, while these terrible trials are occupying all minds."

Judge Corwin made no answer, but lounged carelessly up to a little table at the back of the veranda, which held a massive silver punch-bowl, richly chased round the brim with a pattern of roses and lilies of natural size. This bowl stood upon a salver of the same costly material and ·workmanship—a wreath of corresponding roses and lilies being enchased round the outer border. He lifted the heavy silver ladle, with the family arms richly engraved upon the handle, and dipping up a very moderate portion of the lemon-punch, which was then the common and uncriticised noonday beverage of gentlemen, he put it into one of the tall glasses, whose slender stems were curiously enriched with a white spiral substance artfully blown into the glass, which stood in readiness to receive it; took a sip, and then returning, glass in hand, drew a chair and seated himself near his sister, who had now quietly resumed her embroidery.

"You certainly do brew better punch than any body else, Sister Hannah," he said, approvingly. "I do not get it nearly so good at my own house as you make it."

"That may be because I make it by the old home receipt," said Mrs. Browne, smiling. "I make it just as I used to make it at father's—only the colonel and his father both like it better made of green tea; that is the only change I have made. But won't you stay and dine with us, brother?".

"I don't know—perhaps so. What have you for dinner? Don't put me off with pudding and beans again."

"No, no!" said the hostess, laughing. "I remember that; but it is not baked-bean day to-day—it is Saturday."

"Oh, true. Then, of course, I am to conclude it is to be salt-fish, beef-steak, and apple-pie."

"Of course it is—and will you stay?"

"Yes, thank you, I think so; for my wife is in Boston at her mother's. Here, you little ones," he said, as two of his sister's children came up from the garden and stood at the bottom of the steps looking at him, "run and see if you can find Jim or Sambo, or somebody or other to pull off my boots, and bring me slippers."

When this accommodation had been furnished him, he held out his hand affably to the two little ones, who had returned, and who now stood, hand in hand, at the foot of the steps, silently regarding him, the strict etiquette of the times forbidding a nearer and more familiar approach to their uncle until such time as he might see fit to address them.

"Here, sirrah!" he said at last, addressing the boy, who was the eldest of the two children, "and you, too, little maid Mary, come up here, and tell me what you have learned since I saw you last. What do you know now?—tell me."

"Nothing much, I think, uncle," said the boy, lifting his clear eyes to the inquirer's face, with a look of roguish meaning, as the two stood at their uncle's knee; "I guess I know but little, and sister Mary here don't know any thing." The timid little Mary turned her eyes upon him deprecatingly, but said nothing.

"Well, my little man," said the judge, laughing, as he pinched the boy's round cheek, "that is modest, Johnny, any way. And now, if you please, tell me the little you do know. Hey, sirrah?"

"I know," said the boy stoutly, "that you are one of the judges that are trying the wicked witches, uncle."

"Ahem !" said the magistrate, settling his laced neck-tie, and somewhat disconcerted by the unexpected answer. "Oh ! you know that, then, do you ? And now your turn, my little maid — tell me, if you can, what you don't know."

Raising her clear, soft eyes to his face, the child without a moment's hesitation replied, "I don't know what you will do with all the poor witches, uncle."

"Good !" said the questioner, turning to his sister. "I could not have answered the questions better myself. Your children are quick-witted, and appear to be well posted up in the topics of the day, Sister Hannah."

"Only too much so," said the mother with a sad sigh ; "it is no subject of congratulation to me, I assure you, Jonathan. — You may go now, my children. I wish to talk with your uncle. You and Mary may play in the garden till dinner-time, Johnny ; but do not go down to the water." As the little ones wandered away among the flowers, Mrs. Browne arose and carefully shut the glass doors behind her, and looked anxiously up

at the closed windows. Then resuming her
seat by her brother's side, she spoke in low
tones, but in a voice of deep feeling:

"You say my children are well posted up
in the news of the day, Jonathan, and I regret to confess it is so. It is a solemn and
a fearful thing to have children as young as
these listening to all the details of the horrors that are going on around us. It is a
fearful thing to have their young ears con-
taminated, and their innocent hearts hardened by such things as are the common topics of conversation; and, situated as I am, I
am powerless to prevent it. They hear it
on every hand. I went into the garden only
this very week, and there I found John
Indian and Tituba in close and earnest con-
fabulation with my own servant; and close
by them stood my innocent children, eagerly
listening with open mouths and ears to the
pestilent communications — swallowing all
they heard, and doubtless with their imag-
inations all at work, conjecturing even worse
than they heard from hints and gestures, and
wild, suggestive grimaces; and yet what can
I do to prevent it?"

"Order them off of your premises at once and forever—or get your husband to do it —and forbid their coming again," said the magistrate, unhesitatingly. "Or, if you wish, I will do it for you."

"Oh! no, no!—not for the world. Alas! I dare not—it is a time of too much peril. The very air is heavy with danger, and sickening with horror. I feel that I am in the midst of spies and eavesdroppers," she said, glancing fearfully up at the closed windows, and dropping her voice to a still more cautious whisper. "One knows not where to look for treachery now. My power over my own servants is gone, and I am at their mercy. A chance-dropped word, innocent as it may be, may be caught up and twisted from its meaning, and carried to those who will know how to make a fearful use of it. It has come to this, brother, that I, a quiet, home-keeping matron—a believing, and, I hope, a consistent Christian — connected by birth and marriage with the best and most influential families in the land—I, the daughter of Judge George Corwin, and the wife of the Honorable William Browne, dare not, in my own house, to speak my own mind or order my own servants, lest I should draw down a fearful vengeance on myself or my dear ones. I can not bear it any longer. I seem to be stifling in this dreadful atmosphere; and it was this in part that I wanted to tell you, Jonathan—I have made up my mind to leave the country."

"Good heavens! Hannah; what do you mean? Where will you go?"

"Home to England. My husband has duties that will call him to the court of St. James—you know he has been out before —and he has promised to take me and my children with him. If, by the mercy of God, this horrible cloud is ever dispersed, I will return—if not, I will remain there. Our fathers left England to enjoy freedom of conscience, and the liberty of thought and speech, and we have been taught to honor them for it. I will go back in pursuit of the same inestimable blessings."

"And does your husband approve of this step?" asked her brother, in surprise.

"He consents to it."

"But, my dear sister, this decision of

yours appears to me premature—at least, I think you are nervous and causelessly alarmed. What possible danger can reach you, secure as you are in your social and moral position ?"

" Not more secure than others have be-lieved themselves to be, Jonathan. Oh, my brother ! think of Mrs. Nurse—the purest, truest, humblest Christian ; of high standing in the Church, and blameless in character. I knew her well. She was with me in many of my trials—she was at the birth of all my children ; and in the dark days when it pleased God to take my precious ones from me, she was with me, sustaining my weaker faith and trembling spirits under sickness, suffering, and loss, by her more fervent piety and gentle ministrations. Oh ! I knew her well ; no child ever turned to its mother in surer confidence of finding the support and sympathy it needed than I did to her, and she never failed me ; and where is she now ? Snatched from the home of which she was the loved and loving centre ; reviled and deserted by the neighbors she had served and blessed ; excommunicated by

the Church of Christ, of which she had long
been an honored member; her innocent life
lied away by malicious tongues; she was im-
prisoned for months; she met a felon's death;
and her poor remains are not even allowed
to rest in hallowed ground. Oh, brother!
forgive me if I speak too strongly, but my
heart is full of bitterness; and how do I
know if, before another week closes, I may
not myself occupy the cell from which she
has gone, and my little children be cast out
to the mercy of the cold world, as so many
other poor children have been?"

For a few moments Jonathan Corwin sat
meditating in gloomy silence, his head resting on his hand, while Mrs. Browne wept
silently.   At last, raising his head, he asked
in trembling tones:

"Hannah, do you blame me; do you hold
me responsible for all this? if you do, you
must look upon me as a murderer."

"No, Jonathan," answered his sister, lay-
ing her hand kindly upon his, "I do not
mean to blame you; I know that your office
has its painful duties; I do not believe you
ever willfully wronged any one; but I do

think that you are blinded and deceived; you are my own brother in the flesh, and still more the dear brother of my affections, and I know your heart is a good and true one; it grieves me to differ from you—but I must bear my honest testimony to you that I think you are misled in this matter. I know something of these girls—these 'accusers,' as they are called: I have known Abigail Williams ever since she first came here, and I know her to be an artful, designing, false-hearted girl; I know, too, that Elizabeth Hubbard, the niece of Dr. Griggs his wife, and I know no good of her whatever; and Ann Putnam, too, she has always been known to be a mischievous, malicious girl; I know, too, a little about Mary Warren and Sarah Churchill — Sarah, indeed, lived with me a little while, and I dismissed her for lying. I believe they are both moved by revenge for fancied wrongs against their employers. I know also that for months past, indeed all through the winter, these girls have been practicing all manner of charms and enchantments, all sorts of sorceries and black arts, under the teaching of those Pagan slaves of Mr. Parris—until their brains are overset, and their sense of right and wrong is wholly perverted.

"I do not dare to say how far their sufferings and fits are real or assumed. How far they are acting a part I can not tell, of course; but I do believe that if they are not insane, they are themselves bedeviled.

"I can not understand why their testimony is so freely taken, while that of others is rejected; these insolent, artful girls, whose flippant and reviling tongues are dealing death so recklessly—who are boldly clamoring against lives worth far more than their own—why are they entitled to such credence? Tell me, my brother, do our laws condemn one without allowing him a chance to defend himself? and yet, it is well known, these unhappy prisoners are not allowed counsel; they are not allowed to speak for themselves, unless it is to confess, and all witnesses in their favor are set aside—is this right, is this impartial justice, is this English law?" and she paused.

"Tell me," she said, trying to speak more calmly, "do you get on any? do you see any light breaking in upon this horrible darkness?"

"No," replied the magistrate, sadly; "I must confess I do not."

"Have there been any more arrests or commitments?"

"Several."

"Any new condemnations?"

"Alas! my sister—do not ask me."

"I must ask, Jonathan, and you must hear me. Oh, my brother! remember that the sword of justice is a fearful thing—it is a two-edged weapon, too, Jonathan; beware, lest it turn in your grasp and wound the hand that wields it."

"I do not understand you, Hannah; how do you mean?"

"I mean that this terrible power, thus encouraged and helped on by the ministry, the law, and by medical science, is growing daily more and more exacting; do you fail to see that the victims it demands are daily more numerous and of a higher class in life?—tell me, brother, what will you do if they should accuse your wife or me?"

"Nay, my dear sister, you jest—that can not be—it is impossible."

"Not so; we may be cried out upon any day, any hour; what would you do? Would you believe their accusations against us?"

"Good heavens! Hannah—how can you ask it? No! ten thousand times no! God forbid."

"But why not, if the evidence were conclusive? you have believed it in other cases, why not in ours?"

"Why not? because it would be too monstrous; because I know you both incapable of such things."

"Perhaps so; but how would that avail us? you could not convey your convictions of our innocence to other minds. So did I fully believe in the entire innocence of my poor old friend, Goody Nurse—and so did hundreds of others—but what did that avail her? At my urgent request my husband drew up a paper in testimony of her worth and her blameless life, and many of our best people signed it gladly; but the petition of her friends was rejected, and the words of those miserable children, and of one or two other persons who were known to have a grudge against her or her family, took away her life. Oh! I shudder when I contemplate the widespread misery, the sea of blood that lies before us;—when shall it end?"

"But what can be done, Hannah? I, for one, am open to conviction; suggest a better course."

"I would give the accused a fairer trial; I would have them have counsel to defend them—their very ignorance and helplessness demand it. Think of that miserable Sarah Good, a poor, forlorn, friendless, and forsaken creature, deserted by her husband, the subject of universal prejudice, an object of compassion, not of persecution, surely. I have heard there was not a word brought against her in the whole trial that ought or would have sustained the charge in the mind of any impartial person at a less exciting time; (forgive me, brother; I take my account of these trials second hand—of course, I can not be present myself); and still more, think of her child—that little, miserable, half-starved Dorcas; just think of the whole majesty of the law setting itself against the wits of a poor, little, ignorant, vicious, base-born child, not yet five years old; think,

Jonathan, younger than our little Mary here!
—does it not seem pitiful? it is too un-
equal; if it were not so tragic, it would be
an absurdity."

"But, Hannah, that child was a pestilent
little wretch as ever breathed; if you had
only heard her vile profanity and inso-
lence."

"I do not question it in the least: poor,
miserable little thing, she could be no less—
a vagabond from her very birth; dragged
round from place to place by her vagrant
mother, what chance had she to learn any
thing but evil? Poor little Dorcas! how
often I have fed, and clothed her with my
children's clothing; if I had not, I think her
wretched little body must have perished
long ago—I almost wish it had, it would
have been better for her, perhaps."

"But, Hannah! you know the miserable
child confessed."

"Confessed? yes, I dare say she said just
what she had been told to say—she did not
know right from wrong; but, Jonathan, if
you had been a mother of many children, as
I have been, and had sat and listened, as I

have done, to their thoughtless babble, you would surely have been astonished at the strange and monstrous absurdities that they will often utter."

"Aye, but this child was precociously evil —she was just like her mother."

"And who else should she be like? She never knew any other parent."

"Very true; and 'black cats have black kittens,' they say."

"Sometimes they do, but not always, I believe," said his sister. "And even when they do, I suppose it is from a law of their nature, not their choice."

"Perhaps; but the result is the same, I conclude."

"Pardon me, no! Physically, not morally, it may be the same. In the one case it would be a misfortune simply, in the other it would be a fault."

"Why, Hannah! what a casuist you are! There has been a mistake in our family. You should have been bred to the law, not I."

"Thank Heaven! I was not," said Mrs. Browne, fervently.

"You have reason to say so in these present times," said her brother, sadly. "But you seem to have reasoned upon these matters a great deal. Will you tell me what conclusion you have come to?"

"I am but an ignorant woman, Jonathan —wholly unskilled in all these subtle questions. I never, indeed, thought of these things before; but I can not shut my eyes or close my mind to the terrible realities that are going on around me. I have suffered deeply, and thought much, and of course I have formed my own conclusions."

"And will you not let me have the benefit of them?"

"You put me to the blush, brother. You are a magistrate, and I know nothing of the law."

"But I think the instincts of a pure and earnest, healthful mind are the voice of a higher law—the voice of God. Tell me, then—surely you believe in the existence of the devil?"

"Of course I do. I must. The Bible affirms it, and our Lord Jesus Christ his words do so instruct us. I do believe in persons being bedeviled; but that does not, to my apprehension, imply a belief in witch-craft."

"But where do you make the distinction ?"

"It seems to me that it is a very plain one. It is this: If the devil hath power, which we dare not deny, surely the Lord God Almighty hath a greater power. I think a person may, by his own act, by means of his own sins, forsake God, and be brought into bondage to the power of the devil. Such a one is bedeviled. But I do not believe the devil hath power to take possession of any innocent soul that trusts in God, and make use of it to torment others; and that, as far as I understand it, is witchcraft—being a witch, having power from the devil to torment and bewitch others."

There was silence for a moment, and then Justice Corwin rose, and grasping his sister's hand warmly, he said, "I think, Hannah, if you will allow me to change my mind, I will not dine here to-day. What you have said has given me much to reflect upon. I want the quiet of my own study."

"But, brother, my husband has just come home. I hear the footsteps of his horse at the door. His hospitality will be wounded if you should leave his house just at the very dinner hour. Do stay, and take a hasty dinner with him. He is too busy himself just now to tarry long over the table. Stay, and we will speak of these terrible things no more. You can talk to him about his vessels, his farm, his garden; but do not go until after. dinner. You will oblige me if you will stay."

CHAPTER XII.

CONDOLENCE.

"No! had all earth decreed that doom of shame,
I would have set, against all earth's decree,
The inalienable trust of my firm soul in thee."

MONG all the various members of the community that had been shocked and saddened by the tragical death of Rebecca Nurse, possibly no single individual out of the circle of her own immediate family felt it more keenly or sorrowed more deeply than Alice Campbell. The kind, cheerful, generous-hearted old woman had distinguished her by many little acts of affectionate kindness and many tokens of good-will, and the loving heart of the young girl had warmly responded. Alice was naturally affectionate and grateful, and the extremely limited circle of her personal friends had perhaps intensified the love she bore them.

Then, again, it was the first time that the grim skeleton, death, had ever crossed her own horizon, and here he was revealed indeed as the very "king of terrors." There were no mitigating circumstances—no softening of the awful shadow. The words "here to-day, and gone to-morrow," "in the midst of life we are in death," to which she had listened so often, had suddenly taken on a new meaning, and become to her an awful reality.

The glad young spirit of the girl, so new to suffering, was rent alike with grief for her own loss and intense sympathy for the bereaved family, and her own powerlessness to help or comfort them, and she longed at least to assure them of her undiminished love and trust.

One evening she came up the little door-yard of her humble home, with a step so heavy, so slow and lagging, that her listening grandmother, who was waiting for her, did not recognize it, it was so unlike the usual firm, free, bounding step of her child. As Alice entered the room, the old woman looked up and started, shocked at the ghastly paleness of her darling's face.

"Oh, Allie, my ain precious bairn!" she cried. "Oh! what is it, my darlin'? what ha' kim ower ye?"

Alice did not speak, but, sinking down at her grandmother's feet, she laid her head upon the kind knees that had ever been her place of refuge in all her childhood's troubles, and burst into tears.

"Oh, Allie, Allie, my ain sonsie lassie! what—oh, what is it? Dinna ye greet sae sairly. Tell me what it is that's grievin' ye. Is there ony new throuble? Oh, tell me— tell me!"

"Oh, no, no, grandmother!" sobbed Alice, whose hearty burst of tears had relieved her overcharged feelings. "No, there is nothing new; but I think my heart is broken."

"Na', na', my dearie. Dinna say that, nor think it, either," said the grandmother, fond- ly parting the girl's sunny curls, and ten- derly kissing her. "Ye are young, lassie, an' young hearts dinna break when they think they will. Ye will win ower it, my darlin', in time, though it's hard to bear noo. But tell me, lassie, where hae ye been, an' what hae ye met wi', that ha' so cast ye doon?"

“I have been over to Nurse’s Farm, grannie.”

“To Nurse’s Farm, indeed? Ye don’t tell me sae. An’ did ye walk it a’ the way there an’ bock? Ah, weel-a-weel! I dinna wonder an’ ye are a’ used up. Ye are na’ fit to be gangin’ sae lang a walk.”

“Oh, it was not that, grandmother,” said Alice, relapsing into tears again. “I did not mind the walk.”

“To Nurse’s Farm?” repeated the old woman. “Oh, Allie, my dearie, how could ye hae the heart to go there?”

“Say, rather, how could I have the heart to keep away,” answered the sobbing girl. “Think how kind·and good she was to me, and how much I loved her; think, too, what they have suffered. Oh, how could I keep away, and let them think I believed all those lying, infamous charges?—think that I did not love her, and sorrow with them? Oh, I could not keep away; and though to go has almost broken my heart, still I am glad I have been.”

“I believe ye, dear. It wa’ a hard thing to do; but ye wa’ right to go. Tell me aboot it, Allie.”

"Oh, grandmother, it was sad! sad!—
sadder even than I expected it would be.
Every thing was so changed since I was
there last, and that only so short a time
ago." Alice paused a moment to recover
herself, and then went on.

"You know when I went there last, it was
all so bright and gay. The doors and windows were all set wide open, and the merry
little children were trooping in and out all
the time, laughing and playing, and all the
family were gathered there, so glad and
happy, and all seeming so secure. The very
house seemed to be full of sunshine and
laughter; and now—oh, such a sad contrast! It seemed to me as if I could have
told from the very look of the house outside
that she had gone, and they were mourning
for her.

"Every door and window was shut fast.
Not a creature to be seen moving about—
no happy children, no merry voices, no
laughter, no sunshine. It seemed the stillness of death. I scarcely dared to go in.
Two or three times I lifted the knocker;
but my heart failed me, and my hand fell,

and I did not knock; but at last I did, and
the sound came back to me so hollow and
strange that I thought the house must be
deserted and empty.

"There was a long silence, and then I
heard the shuffling of feet inside, and old
Landlord Nurse himself opened the door for
me. Oh, grandmother! I thought I should
scream when I saw him; he is so changed,
you would not know him—his flesh has all
fallen away; he is sunken, and all bent over
on a cane, and his eyes looked so glassy and
bewildered and winking, as if he had wept
the very sight out of them."

"Puir auld mon! I dare say; I suppose
he is jist fairly dementit wi' the sorrow."

"I could not speak a word to him—I only
held out my hand to him, and broke down,
crying. I could not help it; but I think he
knew me, and knew what I felt, for he
squeezed my hand hard in his, and laid the
other on my head; and then without a word
he led me into the room where his daughter
Sarah was sitting all alone, and oh! so sad.
She held out her arms to me, and I tried to
tell her what I felt, but we both broke down,

and cried together; and the poor old man went into the other room, and sat down in his big chair, and rested his head on the top of his cane, and never spoke or looked up.

"And then, when we had got a little more composed, she tried to tell me about her mother; but every time she tried to speak of her her voice choked, and she cried so terribly, I begged her not to speak of her; and I tried to talk to her of other things—of her father, her sisters, the children, the garden, the poultry—but somehow or other, every thing seemed to lead round to her mother again.

"At last her sisters came in, and I was thankful they did, for they were more composed. I suppose they may have loved their mother as well as she did—perhaps they did; but of course they do not miss her so much, for they have their own houses and their husbands and children to interest them; but poor Sarah is the youngest, and has always lived at home with her, and of course she must miss her the most.

"But when she went out to get the old man's supper ready for him, the others told me all they could about their mother—how patient and resigned and forgiving she was; and, oh! grandmother! this is a great secret—but they told me I might tell you, and I am sure you will be glad to know—they have got their dear mother's body, and buried it decently in their own grounds, and that is such a comfort to them.

"They told me all about it—how one of their kind neighbors kept watch to see what was done with it, and came and told them; and how they all gathered together at their father's house, and the sisters remained with poor Sarah, who was almost beside herself, while their poor old father, with all his sons and sons-in-law, went off at midnight to that awful place to try to recover it. Oh! it would make your heart ache to hear them tell of it.

"There they sat, they said, all alone in the dark, for they did not dare to have a light at that hour in the house, fearing some one might see it and inform against them, or it might betray the party going out or coming home. And so there they sat in the darkness, holding each other's hands, weeping and praying, it seemed, they said, as if it was hours and hours.

"But at last they heard the slow steps of the father and brothers returning, and they knew by their heavy, solemn tread that their search had been successful; and sobbing but silent, they all hurried out and opened the door to give her a sad welcome to her home once more, though they knew it was but for a few hours; and they said, terrible as it was, they were thankful even for that.

"And then the young men went out again and dug the grave in their own ground; and they, her daughters, with their own trembling, loving hands, hastily made her ready for it. And when all was prepared, they all went out together, and placed her there in silence and darkness; not a word was spoken, but they all knelt and prayed silently—for who could tell who might be listening; they did not even dare to raise up the sods above her, lest their enemies might suspect, and steal the body from them; and so they just smoothed it off, and got back to the house just as day dawned. And the young men have taken turns to watch there every night, but it has not been disturbed. And when I was coming away, they took me round to see where they had laid her; but they told me not to pause or even turn my head as we passed the spot, for fear it might betray it, for they think her enemies may still be on the watch to steal her away.

"And so they came with me to the gate, and kissed me, and thanked me for my sympathy, and I came away; but I am glad I went, grandmother, sad as it was."

"Yes, I am sure ye maun be; if it wa' hard to do, it wa' the mair merit—'no cross, no crown'—an' sure an' sartin they maun ha' felt thankful to ye."

"Yes; I am sure they were pleased and grateful for my visit. But, grandmother, I have got something more to tell you—something which seems very strange to me."

"Weel! an' what wad that be, Allie?"

"As I was coming home, walking through the village, thinking sadly of all I had just seen and heard, I heard my own name spoken on the other side of the street—I was sure I was not mistaken—'There, that is the Campbell girl,' I heard the voice say. 'That is Alice Campbell, now.'"

" Haith ! ye wa' mistaken, lassie—ye wa' thinkin' of ither things."

" No, I could not be mistaken—I heard it plainly. You will see I was not mistaken, for as I looked over across the street (I could not help doing that, of course, hearing my own name spoken out so), there stood two women, and one of them was one of those dreadful, lying accusers."

The sensitive young girl stopped and shuddered ; her naturally clear mind had doubted the charge of witchcraft—even when its victims had been vagrants of a more than questionable reputation. But when the awful charge had been brought against her own old friend, whose true and consistent piety and excellence she had intimately known and admired, the whole baseness and falsity of the charge seemed to stand out in bold prominence to her, and she hesitated not to deny the whole thing as an imposture; the cruel injustice of her doom, so opposed to all law, human or divine, which reached out hands eager to secure the victim, had outraged her feelings, and she looked upon the cruel accusers as murderers of her friend.

"But, an' who were they, Allie?" asked her grandmother, as Alice paused.

"I do not know her name—I do not think I ever heard it, though she was pointed out to me as one of them; and the other, an elder woman, was her aunt—I have seen her with her before. When I looked round, the girl called to me, and beckoned with her hand: 'Alice Campbell! come over here; we want to speak to you.'

"But when I saw who it was, and remembered how those lying lips had falsely sworn away the life of my dear old friend, I could not bear to speak to them, or even look at them; I shook my head, and hurried on. In a moment they had crossed the street, and I heard their footsteps hurrying after me.

"'Stop, Alice Campbell,' says the girl; 'I want to speak to you.'

"'I can not stop,' says I; and I almost ran on.

"'Well,' says she, catching my sleeve, 'I must say you're civil; we will walk with you.'

"'I do not care for company,' says I; 'and I am in a hurry.'"

"Oh, Alice, my child! wa' it safe to offend them? Who kens what harm they may do ye?"

"I know it, grandmother; but I could not bear to look at them or speak to them, or have them touch me; I felt as if they were murderers—that there was blood, innocent blood, on their cruel hands.

"'Why do you walk?' says she; 'if you are in such a hurry, why don't you ride?'

"'You might have been riding in your own coach,' says the woman, 'if your old grandmother had not stood in your way.' And then they both laughed.

"'You know nothing of me or my grandmother,' said I. 'Let me go, will you?' and I pulled away my sleeve.

"'Don't I? indeed!' says the woman; 'maybe I know more of her than you do. And when did you hear last from your father, my dear?'

"'You have mistaken me for some one else,' says I, 'for I have no father.' And I broke from them.

"'No; none to speak of, you mean,' says the woman, laughing; but I would not hear any more—I broke from them, and fairly ran down the street. But what did it all mean, grannie?—was it not strange?"

. Could Alice have seen her grandmother's averted face in the gathering twilight, she would have been struck with its sudden change—the ruddy complexion was ashy pale.

"An' hoo should I ken?" she answered angrily, snapping out the words with sharp bitterness; "I did na' see her."

"But what could she have meant?"

"Her meanin'? don't ye ken well enough that they are awfu' liars?"

"But you know who the woman is, I suppose?"

"An' hoo should I? If she is ane of those vile creatures, I wad na' wish to ha' ony thing to do wi' her."

"Oh! but I thought you might have known something of her at home years ago, because she is a Scotch woman, and came out in the spring. Her name is Evans, I think, and I heard she had been making many inquiries about us—so I thought it was possible it might be some one you used to know at home. But never mind about her now. I am all tired out, grandmother, and I think I will go to bed now—it has been a very hard day to me. I am weary all over, in body and mind; I do not think there is a bone in my body that does not ache, and my head and heart the worst of all; I hope I shall feel better to-morrow—and so good-night, grandmother."

And Alice kissed her fondly and left her; but for hours after, Goody Campbell sat silent and motionless, just where Alice left her. But if she moved not, her restless thoughts roved far and wide in vivid recollections of the past; which, if the working of her features might be regarded as indicative of their nature, were any thing but satisfactory.

CHAPTER XIII.

THE MIDNIGHT TERROR.

"In the cold, moist earth they laid her, when the forest cast
    the leaf,
And they wept that one so beautiful should have a life so
    brief."

NEARLY a week subsequent to the conversation between Justice Corwin and his sister, which has been given in a previous chapter, Colonel William Browne, who had found himself strangely vexed and hampered in every way in his business, owing to the excitement of the times, and the intense, all-absorbing interest taken by all classes of the community in the pending witch-trials, informed his wife at "supper-time," as it was then commonly designated, that he should probably be out late, as it was his intention to pass the evening at his father's house, where they were to be busy in adjusting certain shipping-papers relative to the two vessels they were preparing to send out; and requested her, as her health was constitutionally delicate, and her nervous system had been heavily overtaxed of late, not to sit up for him, but to retire at her usual hour; adding, moreover, that as it was wholly impossible for him to say at what hour he might come home, he did not wish any one to be kept up for him, but he would take the key of the side door with him and let himself in, whenever he could get through the business he had on hand.

That night Mrs. Browne was oppressed by a strangely vivid and most uneasy dream. She seemed to be walking by night through a deep and most impenetrable forest, trying to pick her uncertain way through the thick, rank undergrowth which grew up breast-high around and before her; the choking vines and interlaced bushes intercepting and baffling her, clinging ever tenaciously around her feet, and resisting the frantic efforts of her utmost strength to tear them away, while a strangely sweet, but heavy, pungent odor from the branches she bruised seemed to rise and confuse and almost suffocate her, and all the while a strange, weird sound, half tempest, half music, seemed to pursue and surround her.

Gasping, panting, breathless, and oppress-ed, she struggled with this fearful sort of nightmare—now half reviving to conscious-ness, now again sinking down into a sort of conscious stupor, until at length, when the sense of oppression became absolutely un-bearable, she suddenly started and awoke—awoke to the full conviction that some one or something was in the room with her.

For one moment she lay in mute, helpless mental bewilderment, bathed from head to foot with the cold dew of terror, and doubt-ful even where she was—doubtful if she were still asleep or awake — for the closely shut room was too entirely dark to enable her to discover even the faintest outline of familiar things; and still she was conscious of the same warm, sweet, sickening odor, and still sounding in her ears was the same weird, mysterious music; was it in the room or out of it? she could not tell. It was a low, sweet, wailing symphony—unutterably sad;

at times so low as to be scarcely discernible, yet never wholly ceasing: now swelling like the high notes of the Æolian harp, close as it would seem to her very bedside; then softly retreating—away—away—it would seem miles afar, yet still distinct; then swelling again—nearer, and nearer, and yet more near. She was too fearfully agitated, too full of terror, to tell if it were vocal or instrumental—the question did not then even occur to her; it was like a chant by human voices; but if there were words to it, she did not catch them.

At last, with a desperate effort (a very woman's courage, born of excess of fear), she sprang from her bed, and gaining the window with uncertain steps, she loosed the clasp, and flung the casement wide open. The sultry summer night was damp and starless, and although without she could discern the dim outline of the trees, it gave no light into the chamber; but the outer air had somewhat revived her, and for a moment she clung to the window-frame for support, glancing fearfully behind her into the darkness. Nothing moved in the chamber but herself,

the strange music had died away into silence, and in the awful stillness she could
hear the fierce beating of her own heart—
beat, beat, beat! She felt as if the life-blood
thus violently pumped up must break in
hemorrhage over her parched and stiffening
lips.

Another desperate effort, and she has darted across the room and gained the chamber
door. She will call for help; her trembling
hand is feeling for the latch; she has found
it—she has torn it open; a figure stood just
beyond the threshold, and, with a wild, glad
cry—" Oh, William !"—she was springing
forward to the shelter of her husband's arms
—but, merciful heavens! that tall, vague,
shrouded figure, dimly revealed to her by
the hall window just behind him, is not her
husband! not her husband's the cold, damp,
clammy hand that firmly clutched her wrist,
and held her one moment forcibly in the
doorway, then sternly thrust her back into
the chamber, closing the door between them.

Quick as thought, with rare presence of
mind, the trembling woman shot the bolt of
the door. One terror at least was thus shut

out; but what might she not thus have shut in? Clasping her hands about her throbbing temples, "I must not faint," she said mentally; "no, I must not—I must not, and I will not!"

Fully aware that in this terrible emergency she had no one but herself to depend upon, she summoned up all her resolution, and creeping with fearful and uncertain steps in the direction of the fire-place, she groped blindly about for the means of procuring a light.

In those early times, the dangerous but efficient lucifer matches, which we bless and anathematize almost in the same breath, had never been thought of, and thousands who now in moments of need or terror obtain an instantaneous light by a mere scratch upon the wall, have never realized the blessing of this much-abused invention. At the close of the seventeenth century, and long afterward, it was a work of time, skill, and patience to gain a light; and now Mrs. Browne, having found her tinder-box, and secured the necessary apparatus of flint and steel, began to strike a light; but her trembling hands, which shook as in an ague fit, added to the usual difficulties of the task.

A dozen times she struck the implements together nervously before she could obtain a spark, and even when she did obtain it, owing to her trepidation, the tiny messenger of hope fell outside of the prepared tinder in the box, and was lost; another—and another—and they do not light; again it lights, but her own eager, gasping breath has extinguished it.   At length, after repeated disappointments, the tinder is ignited, and she hastily lighted the rushlight at the momentary blaze.   Oh! thank heaven for the protection, the sense of security that there is in light.

She breathed more freely, as looking round the room she saw no traces of disorder or disturbance: every thing was in its place, every thing was unaltered, and this familiar home look did much to compose and reassure her. Finding that the open window had cleared the room of much of its oppressive odor, Mrs. Browne hastened to close and fasten it; and then, as by a natural connection of ideas, she stepped to the other window, which she had not opened — to her surprise she found it unclasped, and a little way opened.

As this window, being situated very near the bed, was rarely opened, this fact confirmed her in the conviction that some one had been in the room. As she hastily shut and fastened it, she heard the side door open and close again—her husband had returned, then. Oh, welcome sound; she recognized his well-known step in the hall below; she heard the familiar creak of the door of the little entry closet where he was wont to deposit his hat and cane; and now his welcome step was on the stairs. Oh! what blessed sense of relief there was in that steadily approaching tread! But then there flashed over her mind the remembrance of that dim, shrouded figure she had seen in the entry way. What if her husband should encounter him, unarmed and in the darkness! and fears for herself all forgotten in tender, wifely anxiety for one so infinitely dear to her, she opened her chamber door and stood, light in hand, to receive him.

"Why, Hannah! why, wife!" said the

strong, hearty, manly voice — "what is the meaning of all this? why in the world are you up at this hour, and with a light? is any one sick?"

Wholly overcome with the sudden reaction of feeling, the overexcited woman put down the light, tottered forward, and sank fainting into his arms.

Colonel Browne was a man of warm feelings, but of a calm temperament; he loved his wife tenderly, but he had often seen her in a fainting fit, to which she was constitutionally subject; therefore he was not alarmed by it, and, remembering the lateness of the hour, he called up no one; bearing her back into her chamber, he found and applied the usual restoratives, which were always at hand, and in a few moments she recovered; and then, sitting with her cold, trembling hands in the firm, warm clasp of his, she told him the story of her terrible experience.

But Colonel Browne, although he listened patiently and respectfully to his wife's narration, was evidently incredulous—husbands are apt to be in such cases. In vain the excited woman reiterated her story: "Pooh,

pooh! sweetheart; it was nightmare—you were dreaming."

"Yes, William, I know; I had had the nightmare, and I had been dreaming, but not then; I was wide-awake enough at the last."

"Well, well, Goody! you see there is nothing in the chamber now, at any rate; you are satisfied of that, I suppose; you must try to go to sleep, my dear Hannah, or you will have one of your dreadful head-aches if you allow yourself to become so much agitated; try to forget it all; it's only a bad dream; we will keep a light burning if you wish, but you will laugh at it all to-morrow—I am sure you will."

Overruled, but not in the least shaken in her own convictions, the mother now insist-ed upon visiting her children's room to see if they were safe, and nothing but the use of her own motherly eyes would satisfy her. Supported on the strong arm of her hus-band—for she was really unable to walk alone—she crossed the entry into the room occupied by the children.

"All safe here, you see," whispered the father, as with carefully shaded light they bent over the little white beds which held their sleeping treasures. "Are you satisfied now, dear Hannah?"

It would have amused a less anxious observer to see how characteristically different the two children were, even in the unconsciousness of sleep—the little, gentle Mary, straight and fair as a lily in her almost breathless repose, with quiet limbs all properly disposed in unconscious grace, a half-formed smile on her calm, sweet face, and her little dimpled hands crossed lightly over her bosom, lay like some saintly fair marble effigy upon a monumental stone, as if sleep had surprised her at her innocent devotions; while the more decided, active Johnny, restless and energetic even in his sleep, with upturned face and eager lips apart, the soft, loose curls brushed back from his moistened brow and flushed cheeks — with graceful limbs tossed about the bed in careless freedom—lay with his little sturdy fists doubled-up like a prize-fighter above the disordered bedclothes, as if he had fought to the very last against the approaches of the slumber that could alone have power to subdue his active nature. Pressing a light but fervent kiss upon the brow of each of her darlings, the mother returned to her own room.

Once more within the sacred privacy of their own apartment, the wife made a new attempt to convince her husband of the truth of her own convictions, but in vain; his incredulity was impenetrable at every point, and she had no proof to offer him beyond her own word and her own firm belief. She called his attention to the fact of the window which she had found open; but to him that fact offered no proof at all.

"Did you look at it before you went to bed, Hannah? Are you quite sure it was fastened then?"

No; she had not looked at it, as it was a window very rarely opened.

"Then," said he, "the fact of finding it open clearly proves nothing; it may have been, and very possibly had been, unfastened for some time past, and you had not noticed it—that is all."

"Then you do not believe in what I have told you?" said the wife.

"I do believe in every word of it, my dear Hannah—that is, I believe in your belief; but I can not share it. I found you in a very nervous, excited, and hysterical state when I came in—this you will allow, certainly—and you tell me you were comparatively calm then, because the light had revealed to you that there was no one in the room. If, then, you were still more excited before I came, how can I help feeling that your judgment was at the mercy of your terrors? It seems to me there is really nothing in all this to prove to my senses that it was any thing more than a distempered dream."

"But you seem to forget, William, that I had the evidence of nearly all my senses," said Mrs. Browne. "You forget that I heard the music, that I smelt the sickening odor, that I saw the veiled figure in the hall, and felt his rude grasp upon my arm. What further evidence of my senses could I have?

"William," she said, after a moment's pause, "I will not ask you further to believe me, for I see that you are wholly incredulous, and I have, as you say, no actual proof to give you. I can not make you believe against what you call the evidence of your senses, and I can not hope to convey to your mind the convictions of my own. But this much I may and I do ask of you: Do not attempt by reasoning or by ridicule to combat what I in my own secret soul fully believe. I do not, I can not attempt to account for the transactions of this night; but my conviction of their reality is as firmly fixed as is my belief in heaven; and your arguments, however much they may wound and distress me, can never convince me.

"Let this subject, then, be dropped between us now and forever. I shall keep my belief until my dying day, and you may keep your unbelief as long as you can; but I do ask that the matter shall never be divulged to friend or foe. If it has come from the invisible world (it may be a warning—I know not), we are, of course, powerless to contend against it; if it is (as it may be) the result of earthly malice, our only safety is in silence. I am too well aware that I have already given offense to the evil ones who seem to rule the hour, by the earnest zeal that I have manifested in behalf of my

poor old friend, Goody Nurse.　I feel that
I am watched and suspected—the merest
trifle, a chance word, a look even, may place
me in the same position.　Complete silence
and total inaction are, I feel, my only chance
for escape, until you can take me and our
children away.　My only hope of safety is in
being overlooked and forgotten.　Will you
not promise me this, at least ?　I ask it for
our children's sake as well as my own."

Of course this promise was freely given;
for Colonel Browne saw, no less clearly than
his wife did, that in the present inflammable
state of the public mind, any notoriety—
any thing which might serve to draw attention to them—would be not only unwise,
but positively unsafe; and he felt sure that
a public discussion of the mysterious events
of the night—in the strange truth of which
his wife so fully believed—would be sure to
link her name with the powers of darkness
in a way that might peril her reputation,
her safety, and even her life; and he fully
agreed to her proposal to keep the whole
affair a profound secret.

In compliance with this decision, Mrs.

Browne, the next day, although she was in reality ill from the effects of her midnight terror, made an effort to rise and appear at the early breakfast-table as usual; but her husband did not tell her that the morning's light had revealed to him that the flowering vines around the porch, beneath the window she had found open, were slightly but discernibly broken, trampled, and crushed, as if an expert climber had ascended and descended by that means; for he feared such a confirmation of her story would only lend a new intensity to her belief; and he fondly hoped that time and change — absence from the terrible scenes around her, and the charms and incidents of foreign travel, to which they were looking forward — would obliterate it from her mind. But in this hope he was mistaken; the conviction was far too firmly rooted, and she brooded over it in fearful silence day and night.

Although in advance of her times in regard to the subject of witchcraft, and looking with scorn and horror upon the mad fanaticism of the multitude around her, she was not, of course, wholly superior to the almost universal superstition of the age she lived in. If the occurrences of that fearful night —which seemed burned in upon her heart and brain—were natural or supernatural, she could not tell; either way they boded her no good, and they haunted her.

It might be that the terrible secret was all the more terrible to her because she kept it so closely locked up in the recesses of her own breast. She received no sympathy, for she asked none. Between herself and her husband her own wish had made it a forbidden subject, and no one else knew of it—not even to her brother, Judge Corwin, whom she tenderly loved, and with whom through life she had ever been in the habit of full, free interchange of thought and feeling, did she ever in any way allude to the secret weight of gloomy apprehension which was slowly but surely dragging her downward to an untimely grave.

Her naturally delicate, nervous organization could not long bear up against so intense a pressure, and her health gave way. Slowly at first, and almost imperceptibly, but daily more and more speedily, the sad change came; and as the summer drew near to its close, she drooped more and more. There were indeed—as there often is in these cases—alternate intervals of failure and of recruit; but those who watched her most closely and most tenderly saw that when she rallied, she never got back to the point she had last failed from.

The purposed trip to the mother country had to be given up, for she had not now the strength to make the passage as it was then obliged to be made.

People called it a decline—perhaps it was so; but, though gentle as ever, she never revealed her solemn secret—possibly her husband thought she had forgotten it.

The most skilled physicians were called in, but the case baffled their highest art; for she alone knew what had sapped the springs of life, and she would not tell.

The sad summer passed on, and as the flowers faded, she faded with them. When the brilliant days of the Indian summer drew near, and the land put on its gorgeous robes of regal beauty, she would sit, propped up in her cushioned chair, at the southern window, which overlooked the garden where her children played, her quiet eyes roaming, with their tender, wistful gaze, over the blue, dancing waters of the little cove to the fair, green hills beyond—or turning dreamily to the golden southwest, where the sunset clouds spread their pavilion curtains of purple and softest rose-tints; and "when the melancholy days had come, the saddest of the year," a shrouded armorial hatchment over Colonel Browne's door, a passing bell, and a slowly moving train wending its mournful way to the then thinly populated burial-ground, told of the removal of one whose youth and health, rank, wealth, beauty, grace, and loveliness are now known only "as a tale that is told."

CHAPTER XIV.

"'Tis well for us there is no gift
Of prophecy on earth,
Or how would every pleasure be
A rose crushed at its birth."

ALICE retired to her bed; but, weary as she was, she could not sleep. Hitherto, whatever her griefs or anxieties had been, night had brought repose—sleep, blessed sleep, that panacea of all human woes, which the young and happy have never learned to estimate, had never failed her before; but now her powers of mind and body had all been overtasked, and her whole delicate nervous system was shaken by the intense strain it had undergone, and she could not sleep. Restless and feverish, she turned from side to side in strange, unwonted wakefulness. Her head ached, her cheeks burned,

her temples throbbed, her aching eyes seemed strained unnaturally wide open, and her
hot hands and restless arms were tossed
wildly above her head.

She had no power to stop the action of
mind and memory. Thought seemed to her
like the great wheel of some ponderous ma-
chine, which, once set in motion, could neither be guided nor stopped, but would go on
and on forever, with its terrible but useless
activity.

Probably, for the first time in her healthy,
happy young life, she realized what wakefulness was, and she lay, with quick beating
heart and widely opened eyes, staring into
the blank darkness, through long, uncounted
hours, that seemed to her inexperience to be
interminable.

Of course, in this state of enforced bodily
stillness, and unnatural mental excitement
and activity, the sad scenes of the previous
day, the terrible sorrow she had witnessed
and shared in could not be put aside—it
was all lived over again in her excited imagination.

Again in memory she went through all

the sad details of that harrowing story; again she saw and pitied the silent, hopeless grief of the bereaved and sorrow-stricken old man, whose voiceless woe was more eloquent than the most expressive words; again she seemed to pass that nameless and unmarked grave, where she dared not pause to drop a tear, and over which the tenderest love ventured not to place a stone or a flower. And when, by a powerful effort of self-will, she at last succeeded in turning her mind away from this dreadful subject—there rose up before her the recollection of her unwilling interview with the two women who had so rudely accosted her in the street on her way home, and she naturally began to wonder who they were and what they could have meant.

She had never spoken to either of them before, and knew nothing of them beyond what she had told her grandmother. What, then, could they know of her or her affairs?

But as Alice pondered this question curiously, a new thought took possession of her mind. The woman had spoken of her father —how oddly the words sounded to her ears

—her father? She had never heard of him before; and, strange as it now seemed to her, when her thoughts were thus turned to the subject, it had never before occurred to her that she ever had a father.

Her grandmother had so constantly spoken of her as her daughter's child, as her own Alice's "wee Allie," that it had never entered her mind that she belonged to any other parent.

Her grandmother, her mother, and herself —these formed for her a regular trio; and she had grown up so impressed with the idea that they three were and had been all in all to each other, that any other relationship had seemed superfluous; but now, when her thoughts had been called to the subject, she wondered at her own stupidity, and puzzled herself in wild conjectures. Why had her grandmother never mentioned her father to her? No doubt he must have died long ago—in her infancy, perhaps, as her poor mother did. And yet, if he had—her grandmother had always talked to her of her mother, and had taught her to love and cherish her memory. Why, then, had she

not taught her to remember and love her
father too?

Surely, she thought, her grandmother must
have done so—of course she had, and she,
undutiful child, must have forgotten it. It
would all come back to her by and by—she
should be able to remember what grannie
had told her about her father; and she taxed
her memory to the utmost to try to recall
any such information—any allusion, even, to
such a person having ever existed. It was
all in vain; but as she thus explored the ut-
termost limits of her childish recollections,
there came up a dim, shadowy remembrance
of that vague suspicion which had been
awakened long ago, when she was but a little child, and had dressed her hair with the
purple flowers, and grandmother had seemed
so displeased with her—she did not know
why. She did not understand it then, and
she did not understand it any better now.
It was all so hazy and dim, she could make
nothing of it.

Turning away in despair from that vain
research, the restless thoughts took a new
direction, and she began to wonder who and

what this unknown father could have been. Already his very name had taken a strong hold upon her innocent affections. Surely she ought to love him, to make up to him for her life-long forgetfulness. Who could he have been? What was he like? What was his name? But here a new question started up—why did not she bear his name, instead of that of her mother and grand-mother?

In vain she questioned and conjectured. There was but one way out of this strange mystery—her grandmother must know all about it. To-morrow she would ask her. Yes; to-morrow she would get her grand-mother to tell her all about it; but though she repeated these words to herself a dozen times, they did not satisfy her impatient longing, and more widely awake than ever, she looked and longed for the coming day.

And Mrs. Campbell, too, had had her sleep-less night (but it was not so new to her). She, too, had been tossing restlessly, striving vainly with the memories of the past and the anxieties of the future.

Again she reviewed the sad events of

other days; again, with a renewed bitterness, they rose up before her; again she strove with a mighty sorrow, a cruel wrong, an unmerited disgrace, a fierce temptation, a ready revenge, a yielding circumstance; again she weighed chances long passed, and pondered probabilities all long gone by, and balanced with trembling hands and wavering brain the eternal right and wrong.

Again she seemed to look with bitter anguish on the face of the dead; again, by her persistent will, she tore open the deep but unforgotten wounds of her heart, and laid her own fierce hand on the unhealed scars that bled with a touch.

Alas! there was no comfort there. What had all that suffering brought her, that a chance word might not have swept away?

She never for a moment doubted that Alice would question her—she knew the girl too well to doubt it. That quick, imperative spirit was too like her own for her to think for a moment that she would relinquish her purpose. How could she baffle or resist her? and what and how should she answer her eager inquiries? What to keep

back, and what to reveal, was a momentous
and unanswerable question. Long and painfully she pondered it, but no new light broke
in upon the troubled darkness of her spirit;
for the trying ordeal must be met, and to-
morrow would surely bring it.

At last she made up her mind that she
would steadfastly refuse all explanation
whatever. Alice could not force it from her,
and she should not. She might, indeed,
question—no doubt she would; but what
then? She had held her own sad secret for
more than eighteen years—should a mere
child have power to wring it from her now?

With this fallacious hope, of the insecurity
of which she was but too well aware, she
tried to fortify herself for the coming interview; but it was with a new and strange
feeling of constraint on both sides that the
grandmother and her child met each other
the next morning.

CHAPTER XV.

ESTRANGEMENT.

"A something light as air—a look—
A word unkind or wrongly taken ;
Oh ! love, that tempests never shook,
A word—a breath—like this has shaken."

IN the silent and lonely hours of the sleepless night it had seemed to Alice a very simple and easy thing to ask the question she meditated, and obtain from her grandmother the information she desired, and she longed for the coming day to dawn that she might begin her investigation ; but in the clear light of day it seemed neither so easy nor so practicable, and she almost trembled at the temerity of her own purpose.

She glanced at her grandmother's stern, set face (all the more stern from her midnight resolve), and her habitual awe and reverence for the old woman came back to her with redoubled force. She saw, too, that her grandmother was watching her with uneasy glances, and her heart sunk appalled at the task she had set herself; yet she never for one moment thought of relinquishing her purpose.

And the grandmother, on her part, noticed Alice's furtive, uneasy glances at her, and knew the dreaded hour was at hand, and braced herself to meet it.

"I laid awake nearly all night last night, grandmother," said Alice, at length, beginning afar off; "I could not sleep for thinking —my visit was such a sad one."

"I dinna doot it," replied Mistress Campbell, gravely. "Ye had a lang, weary walk, an' a varry mournfu' visit; I wad na' wonder ye could na' sleep."

"No, indeed. I seemed to live it all over again—I could not forget it; and I got my eyes so wide open, it seemed as if I should never sleep again. And then, grandmother" —and here, in spite of all her efforts to keep it steady, the poor child's voice trembled a little, and she was sure her grandmother noticed it — "and then I thought of what those women said to me in the street."

“Haith! Alice,” said the old woman, snappishly, as she rose from the table, as if to put an immediate end to the conversation, “an’ what do ye fash yersel’ aboot them for? Ye ken fu’ weel that they are vile leers an’ defamers; dinna talk o’ them to me—forget them—let them gang.”

“Yes, grandmother, I know — I would gladly forget them; I do not wish ever to see or hear of them again. I only want you to tell me what they meant.”

“An’ hoo suld I ken their meanin’ mair than yersel’? I did na’ hear them.”

“No; but I told you what they said.”

“An’ what if ye did? I ha’ nathing to say to them; an’ I dinna care to ken their leeing words.”

“But, grandmother, tell me what it meant.”

“How do I ken? I ha’ nathing to say to them or of them; an’ I suld think, Allie, ye wad na’ care to keep company wi’ them that wrought the death o’ Goody Nurse.”

Trembling with vainly suppressed passion, Goody Campbell uttered these taunting words. She meant that they should cut deeply, and they did; but she saw in a moment that she had made a mistake — she had gone too far. Alice's pale face flushed to the very temples, and all the passionate impulse of the temper she had inherited from her grandmother flashed back upon her from those startled eyes.

"Grandmother, it is not of Goody Nurse or her accusers that I am speaking," she said, controlling her rising temper with diffi-culty, "but of my father."

Goody Campbell made no answer, beyond an emphatic and contemptuous "Hump!"

"I ask you," said Alice, with her blue eyes wide open, and glittering like cut steel— "I ask you only to tell me about my father."

"An' I hae nathing to tell ye. Tak' yer answer, an' gang."

"I will not take that answer. You have told me about my mother a hundred times; then why not tell me something about my father?"

"I dinna ken ony thing aboot him—I hae nathing to tell ye. I hae na' seen him, or heard fra' him, sin' ye kim into the warld. What hae I to tell?"

"Neither have you seen nor heard from my

mother since I was born; and yet you can talk to me for hours about her."

"Alice," said the grandmother, making a desperate effort to re-establish her hold upon the girl's affections, "hoo kin ye try me sae? Yer mither wa' my ain bairn—my on'y child; sure I hae much to tell o' her; an' ye are her on'y bairn. Hoo kin ye doot me? Hoo kin ye doot if I hae ony thing pleasant to tell ye I wad na' wait for ye to question me?"

But the effort failed. Alice stood proud and unyielding.

"Grandmother, I do not ask for pleasure —I ask for information. I have a right to know something of my own history—of my own parents. I have been kept blinded long enough. I am no longer a child, to be put aside with a jest or a scolding. I ask you again—will you tell me about my father, or not?"

Alice paused; but there was no answer.

"Grandmother, I am in earnest; will you answer me—yes or no? I must know the truth."

"Ye maun know, did ye say, Allie?

Haith! lass, 'must' is a bold doggie enow; but 'you can't' is the doggie that kin pu' him doon, an' hold him there, I wot."

"Perhaps so," said Alice, carelessly. "But 'I can and will' can conquer even him, I think; and I tell you now plainly that I both can and will."

"Tut, tut! lass. Dinna bark when ye kinna bite—hoo kin ye, an' hoo will ye?"

"I will go to the women I met in the street; it is clear to me that they know what you refuse to tell me. 'An open enemy is better than a false friend'—I will go to them."

"Alice, girl, are ye mad? Would ye gang to those awfu', leeing creatures that hae the power o' the evil-eye? Ye wad na'—ye wad na'."

"I will," said Alice, calmly; "I fear them not. I will brave the evil-eye, and the evil tongue too—but I will find out the truth you are hiding from me. I will give you the day to make up your mind in—I will wait until the evening; if you choose to tell me then, I will have the story from you—if not, then before this night closes I will try to learn it from them."

“Nay; but Alice, hear me.”

“No,” said Alice, “there is no use in any more angry words. We have both spoken too many already. I will wait till night; then you may speak or not, as you may think best;” and sweeping by her grandmother with an air of proud defiance she had never manifested before, Alice left the room.

During the rest of the day no word was exchanged between this so lately loving pair. In silence they met and passed each other in the performance of their respective daily duties, and in silence each covertly and anxiously scanned the face of the other—but in vain. They were well-matched antagonists, for they were far too much alike in temper and spirit, for either of them to be able to detect one sign of wavering in the other.

But when their evening meal was over, Alice rose in silence and put on her shawl.

“Alice !” cried her grandmother, starting as from a stupor, “where are ye gangin’ the night ?”

“I am going to the village, as I told you I should.”

“Whist ! Alice, girl,” said Mrs. Campbell,

seizing the shawl with no gentle hand, and
drawing it hastily from her shoulders; " ye
are na' gangin' to those awfu' leeing creatures."

" I am," said Alice, resolutely.

" Girl, ye are mad—mad !   I think the
power o' the evil-eye is upon ye a'ready."

" It is your own work, grandmother.   Remember always, if any harm come of it, it
was you that sent me there; it was not my
own choice to seek them—you drove me
to it."

" What is it ye wad know, lass ?" said the
woman, brought to terms at last.

" I want to know the story of my birth
—I want to know about my father; I have
been kept blindfolded long enough.   I want
the whole story—and I want the truth."

" Alice," said the old woman sadly and
reproachfully, " ye are unjust.   For yer' ain
sake — to spare ye — I hae concealed the
truth, that I ken too weel will gie ye sair
pain ; but niver in a' my life did I tell ye a
lee."

" Very well," said Alice, coldly ; " let us
have an end of concealment now.   Will you

tell me the whole story now?—or shall I seek it of others?"

"I will, Alice; but if it gies ye pain, mind ye hae yersel' to thank."

"Very well," said Alice, folding up her shawl and resuming her seat—"I will take that risk."

CHAPTER XVI.

GOODY CAMPBELL'S STORY.

"A coldness dwells within thy heart,
  A cloud is on thy brow;
We have been friends together—
  Shall a light word part us now?"

"YE hae set me a hard task, Alice," began her grandmother; "hard-er far than ye ken, for the story ye ask is sair to hear an' sair to tell; but 'the willfu' mon maun hae his way,' an' if it makes yer ain heart as heavy as mine, ye will remimber ye wad hae me speak.

"It's an ower lang tale, lass—for to gar ye onderstan' hoo it a' came aboot, I maun needs gae far bock, an' tell ye somethin' o' my ain youth. Like yer mither an' yersel', I wa' an on'y child, an', like her too, an' yersel', I wa' called fair to luke upon, an' had a quick, passionate temper—I think these things rin in our bluid.

"My father wa' a mon in humble life, but he wa' a guid mon, an' ane that wa' much respectit; he wa' weel off for his station—he wa' na' so to say rich, but he farmed his own lan'—he had a snug little farm, a sma' housie, a cosy but an' ben, as we ca' it; he owed nae mon a penny, an' he had a little siller laid by, as he used aften to tell me, for my tocher — for he wa' varry fond o' me. An' so it kim aboot that, being called fair, an' my father reputit rich, I wa' na' to seek for suitors; but I did na' care for them—ane an' a' wa' nathing to me.

"But my father's little place wa' near a barrack toon, an' ane day I met wi' a gay young soger laddie fra' the toon—weel-a-weel, lassie, words are but idle brith, never mind them; but he had a merry eye, a ready tongue, an' a winsome smile; an' the upshot o' it wa' that he woo'd an' won me; an' I had nae thought but for my gay, bonnie soger laddie.

"But my father, he wad na' hear tell on't. 'He's but a rovin' blade, Elsie,' he said to me; 'he'll maybe be ordered awa' fra' here ony day in the year, an' then I'll lose my

on'y child.'   An' mair he said to me, an'
mair to the purpose; but, whist! lassie,
young girls are aye silly—an' luve is blin',
an' deaf too; I wa' jist like a colt fra' the
heather, an' I wad na' hear till him.

"'Ye may tell yer braw wooer, Elsie,' he
said to me ane day, 'if he courts ye for the
siller, he wi' marry ye wi' an empty han';
for I tell ye noo that niver a baubee o' my
honest arnings sall gae into his pouch, to be
squandered ower the mess-table; an' ye may
tell him so fra' me.'

"But I did na' tell him—I could na'; I
thought, puir silly lass, that it wa' as if I
dooted his luve; an' so when my father an'
mither baith held out agin' him, an' talked
hard to me about Robin, I jist rinned awa'
fra' them, to follow the fortunes of my gay
soger lad.

"He married me, Allie—yes, he made me
his honest wife; ah! he took tent o' that,
for he counted sure upon my little fortin;
but my father—alas, he better onderstood his
flathering tongue than I did, for whin he
wrote him word that a' his sma' property
wad gae to his brither's son, my husband

cursed me to my face, an' swore I haed cheated him into marryin' a penniless lass.

. "Weel; I trow I haed a hard life enow —but I wa' true to him; for mind ye this, Allie, I wa' his wife, an' I luved him, in spite o' a' his onkindness. So I held by him for ower two years—through guid an' evil—till my little baby wa' born, an' thin jist what my father haed foretold kim true—the regiment wa' ordered to move, an' he went whistlin' awa', an' left me wi' the puir wee thing lyin' by my side, an' na' the first ha'f-penny to live on, an' me too weak to ettle to win ane.

"An' thin—ah! Alice, mind ye, there's nae luve like the luve that ha' growed up wi' us: my father haed niver lost sight o' me, though he left me to drink the cup I brewed; he kim to me in my desolation, an' took tent o' me, an' my puir wee lambie.

"In less than a month I got news o' the shipwreck o' ane o' the transport ships, an' my husband wa' lost. Thin my father an' mither forgave me, an' took me hame to their hearts ance mair; an' whin they deed long after, they left me weel-to-do; an' my wee

Allie wa' to hae it a' after me. An' my Allie, oh! she wa' jist the varry light o' my een; an' sae fair, an' sweet, an' sousie—every bodie luved her; an' she haed luvers too, but she did na' care for ony o' them, she wa' crouse an' cantie as a bird in the tree, but niver bould—jist cannie an' sweet to all.

"There wa' ane chiel, a nee'bor's lad, that coorted her, an' I liked him, an' fain wad I hae married her to him, an' kept her anear me; but it wa' na' sae to be. He wa' an honest, hamely bodie, but Allie did na' tak' a likin' to him. Ye see, she haed been better educatit than ever I were, an' she wa' mair of a leddie—she wa' often up at the manse, an' the rector's young leddies, they made friends o' her, till at last she half lived there, an' there's where the trouble began.

"The rector's son, he haed been tutor to a young mon, the on'y son o' a wealthy English family; they haed been on their travels —he an' his tutor that haed been—an' whin they kim hame, he kim wi' him to the rectory, an' there he an' Alice met—an' she wa' very fair, an' sweet, an' innocent, an' the young mon made luve to her.

"Whin I kim to the knowledge o' it, I wa' sair vexed, for though he seemed an honorable young mon, an' asked her in marriage, an' though I kenned she wa' fair an' good as the varry angels were, an' would be no discredit to ony mon, still I kenned his family wa' rich, an' proud, an' high-born— an' they might feel she wa' na' his equal; an' I wad na' hae my precious child looked doon on by ony o' his English bluid—an' sae I refused to hear till it; an' whin I heard his father wanted him to wed a girl whose father's lands joined his ain, I wa' glad to hear it, for I thought that wad stop it. But I reaped as I haed sowed—my bonnie Alice fled fra' my hame, as I haed fled fra' my father's. Ah! then I kenned what my ain sin haed been; then I kenned what my father and mither haed suffered for me, an' I felt I haed na' a word to say.

"In a day or two mair I got letters, beggin' me to forgi'e them (ah! hoo could I refuse—I that haed dune the varry same thing mysel'?); they wrote me that they were privately married directly Allie left hame; that as the auld laird wa' varry sick, an' it wa’ feared ony vexation or opposition might do him an injury, so it wa’ to be kept secret fra’ him for a while. Ah! lassie, I tell ye I did na’ like the lukes o’ that—but what could I do but try to be patient?

“Weel, time wint on; I got letters fra’ my Alice regularly, an’ she wa’ so happy, her husband wa’ a’ she could ask—an’ I tried to feel satisfied.

“In little mair than a year I got word fra’ her that the auld laird, her husband’s father, wa’ mair dangerous—they feared something wa’ wrong aboot his head, an’ his doctors haed ordered him awa’ for his health, an’ he wad na’ gae without his on’y son went too—an’ as he haed na’ told of his marriage, an’ dare na’, he could na’ be excused. .

“So as Alice wa’ in delicate health, her husband wad na’ lave her amang strangers, an’ he haed gi’en consint she should come hame an’ stay wi’ me while he wa’ gone. An’, oh! she wa’ as blithe as a bird at the thought o’ seeing me, an’ Tibbie, an’ the auld hame again; an’ ye may think I wa’ nae less delightit at the chance to see my bonnie bairn.

"Weel, I made ready for her wi' a glad heart—I an' auld Tibbie, who haed been her nurse, an' luved her a'maist as weel as I did. But a day or twa before she wa' expectit to come, I wa' out to buy some sma' matters, an' I chanced upon Jeannie Evans, the sister o' the lad that I wanted Allie to marry, ye mind, an' I kenned weel she haed na' forgi'en Allie for the slight she felt we haed put upon her brither.

"'Haith! Mistress Campbell,' she says to me, 'this is great news indeed; I. hear tell,' she says, 'yer Allie is kimming hame to ye again. I did na' think,' she says, 'that he'd cast her aff sae sune; it wad hae been better by far for her to hae married to a puir but honest boy, that wad hae stood by her, an' luved an' respectit her, if he were but a hamely lad like Sandie Evans.'

"'An' what do ye mean by that?' I said; though I kenned well eneugh by the evil luke in her wicked een what she meant.

"'Oh!' says she, 'have ye na' got yer een opened yet? My faith! hoo blind people kin be whin they don't choose to see! ye dinna think it is a real marriage yet, do ye—an' he sendin' her aff like this?'

"An' this to be said o' my guid an' beautiful Alice, an' said to her ain mither, too! Oh! I could hae struck the creature to the earth, but I dared na' trust mysel' to answer her. I turned awa' and went hame. I told auld Tibbie, for she luved my bairn a'maist as I did mysel'; an' she counseled me to be silent, an' na' to let Allie ken what we haed heard, an' see wha' she wad say: if it were true, an' she kenned it, she wad be sure to tell us—an' if the puir lassie did na' ken it, why should we be the anes to tell her?

"Weel, she kim; an' oh, Allie, it seemed she wa' mair beautiful than ever; she wa' dressed a' in her rich silks as a leddy should be, an' she haed jewels on her neck an' arms; an', the innocent, loving young thing, she haed dressed her beautiful hair wi' the purple heather flowers, to show me she luved her ain countrie still; an' she wa' a' sae bright an' sae happy, an' sae full o' praises o' her husband—*her husband!* Oh, but it made my varry bluid creep in my veins to hear the innocent creature ca' him so, knowing weel what I did of his vile baseness—but I never let on to her, I took tent o' that.

"Ance or twice, whiles she talked to. us sae glad an' gay, an' lookin' sae bonnie, I thought I saw a strange, sudden luke o' pain pass ower her sweet face; an' at last I took notice o' it, an' I questioned her aboot it. At first she put me by, an' telled me it wa' nathin'; but at last she had to own up, an' she telled us that in gettin' out o' ane o' the coaches on her route hame, she had slipped an' fallen, an' haed somehoo strained hersel' a little; but she tried to laugh it aff, an' said it wa' nathin'; but Tibbie an' I felt there wa' reason to be anxious in her circumstances.

"That night, alas! she haed to ca' us up—oh, that wa' a dreadfu' night! an' before the mornin' broke on us, you, a puir, weakly baby, wa' prematurely born, an' Alice—my treasure, my darlin', my on'y child — wa' gaen fra' me foriver.

"Then, Alice, I think my brain gave way, an' I wa' mad—mad! There wa' but ane bit o' comfort left me—I wa' glad I haed never told her o' the sin o' the mon she luved sae weel; an' she died in her innocent belief that she wa' his luved an' lawfu' wife—

that wa' a comfort as regarded her, the on'y comfort; but as for him, the deceiver—I could hae torn his fause heart out.

"But Tibbie helped me in my thirst for revenge. Tibbie an' I haed been alone in the house wi' Alice—nabodie but she an' I kenned the terrible event of the night. She put it into my mind to conceal yer birth; she took ye, poor unconscious babe, under her plaidie, an' awa' wi' ye to the house o' her brither, who had a baby aboot the same age, an' left ye wi' his wife, who promised to rear ye wi' her ain young ane. Tibbie swore them to secrecy, an' kim bock to me; an' wi' our ain hands we made our darlin' ready for the grave—we were a' alane wi' our dead an' our dool; but if we had na' been, I wad hae let nae hand but my ain or Tibbie's touch her sweet bodie.

"An' so my precious Allie wa' laid in her grave, close by the side o' my father an' mither; an' then the auld rector, who knew an' loved my Alice, who haed baptized her, an' read the burial service ower her, an' who knew a' that the young folks cared to tell him, he wrote out to yer father, at the outlandish place (wheriver it were, I did na' ken) where he an' the auld laird were. I did na' ask him wha' he wrote, an' he did na' ask me wha' he should write; I wa' thankfu' for that. I suppose he thought I wa' too wild like in my great sorrow to send any message; so he jist wrote wha' he thinked best. Nae doot he telled him o' the accident she met wi' on her way hame, and o' its fatal effects, which might weel hae been expectit in her circumstances; but he could na' tell him o' the birth o' her child—nabodie guessed that—nabodie haed seen her fra' the time she kim, till they seen her sweet face in the coffin; nabodie kenned wha' had happened but Tib and I, for the event had na' been expectit for many weeks yet, an' the secret wa' safe eneugh wi' us.

"After a while news kim fra' abroad that the auld mon wa' gainin' somewhat, out there where the doctors haed sint him; an' now that Alice wa' gone, his son's first duty wa' to his father, an' he wad stay wi' him as long as he remained there. The rector telled me this; an' there wa' somewhat aboot luve an' sorrow—idle, bleth'rin words! I did na' care to hear them—they could na' bring bock my bairn to me, or atone for the wrong he haed done her."

"But, grandmother," said Alice, raising her pale face, and speaking for the first time, as Goody Campbell paused—"tell me, what did he, what did my father say, when you did see him? tell me—did he deny or own the terrible wrong?"

"Haith, Alice, I haed nae chance to see him; an' I wad na' if I haed. I ne'er looked on his fause face again; my on'y wish wa' to keep out o' his way."

"But did you never write to him—never question him—never charge him with his baseness? never give him a chance to clear himself?"

"Not I, indeed! Hoo could he repair the wrong he haed done? My bonnie lassie wa' lyin' under the mools; an' wha' wa' he to me? Would I gi'e him the chance, think ye, to cast mair dishonor on my Alice's memory, or to disown her innocent bairn? Never, never! I tell ye, No!"

"But, grandmother, that was unjust. You took the angry word of a revengeful woman against him, and gave him no chance to dis-prove it. That was cruel—cruel and unjust. I will not so lightly accept the story of my mother's shame and my father's dishonor. I will hold fast by the loving trust my sweet mother had in him. But tell me—did he never seek you out when he returned to his home again?"

"He did na' return for years; an' lang before he did come hame, I wa' far eneugh awa'. I wa' too restless an' unhappy to remain there, where every thing reminded me o' a' that I haed lost. I wanted to be awa'—awa' fra' a' that knew me. I sold the little place that wa' my father's, an' removed awa' to the Highlands—to the 'Hillside Farm' —wi' on'y my faithful Tibbie; and there, where nabodie kenned my sad story, where nabodie spiered to ken my name or where I kimmed fra', there I ventured to tak' ye hame to me; for ye wa' a' I haed left to me in life, an' in ye I felt a'maist as if I haed my ain Allie bock again.

"But when ye wa' five or six year auld I·chanced to see by a paper that the auld laird wa' dead, an' that his son wa' comin' hame to England; an’ I could na’ rest easy for the fear he might track me out, an’ tak’ ye fra’ me, ye wa’ so like yer mither; an’ sae I sold a’ out again, an’ took ship, an’ kim to America, for I made sure he’d ne’er find me here.”

“But, oh, grandmother!” said Alice, speaking in quick, eager tones; “is he—is my father—oh! tell me—is he living yet?”

“I dinna ken; I hae telled ye a’ I ken aboot him.”

“And you do not know that he is dead, then?—you never heard that he was?”

“I tell ye I dinna ken aught mair aboot the mon; I dinna want iver to hear o’ him again.”

“But I do,” said Alice, rising proudly; “he is my father, and as such I will love and honor him, until I know he is unworthy of my love. I will seek him the world over, and not until I hear it confessed by his own lips will I believe this cruel story.”

“Ye will seek him, did ye say, Alice? an’ hoo?” asked the grandmother, with a contemptuous smile.

“I will cross the sea to find him, if I have

to work my passage," said the girl, resolutely; "and, if he still live, I am sure I shall find him."

"An' hoo will ye ken where to seek him, silly bairn?"

"I will go first to the rectory—I know how to find my way there. I will tell my story, and those who knew my mother will help her child to find her father."

"An' ye will leave me, Alice?" said the trembling voice of the old woman.

"I will go to my father," replied the resolute tones of the younger one.

"Alice! Alice! an' is this a' the return ye make me for the care that ha' bred ye, an' fed ye, an' luved ye wi' a mither's luve, for mair than eighteen years."

"Grandmother," said Alice, sternly, "I remember only that for more than eighteen years you have deprived my poor widowed father of his daughter's love, and me of a father's love and care."

"An' ye will leave me, an' go to seek the fause-hearted mon that wronged yer puir mither? Oh, Allie! Allie! I did na' luke for this fra' ye."

"Grandmother, you are cruel—cruel! you have no mercy—you have no pity for me! You stab me to the heart, and then ask me for love and gratitude—you have no mercy, none."

As Alice uttered these words, with raised and passionate voice, a slight rustling under the open window attracted Goody Campbell's attention, and fearing they might be overheard, she rose to close the sash; but as she did so, a retreating footstep, and a low, mocking laugh, floated back to her, and convinced her that they had had listeners; but she was too much troubled with the turn affairs had taken to pay much heed to the circumstance. She closed the window, and returning to her usual chair, sat down in ominous silence, her head resting on her hand. And Alice too remained silent, busy with her perplexed and tumultuous thoughts. And so they sat in silence for more than an hour, Goody Campbell absorbed in the past, Alice quite as much absorbed with the future; Alice nervously and restlessly changing her position, while her grandmother never moved.

But Alice, though quick and impulsive in temper, was affectionate and loving; and her heart upbraided her. From time to time she glanced uneasily at the unmoving figure in the old arm-chair. It seemed to her that a strange grayness was stealing over those aged features. Surely she thought, as she looked at her, she had grown old since the morning; and was it her unkindness that had wrought the sudden change?

She thought of all her patient love and tender care; she thought of all she had suffered, and all she had lost—her parents, her husband, her only child; and her warm but hasty little heart swelled in pitying and repentant tenderness. How still she sat, so motionless! oh, if she would only move her head—her hand! And her usually erect figure, how drooping! There was something awful in her unnatural silence and stillness. Oh, what if her unkindness had broken that true and loving heart! what if she were palsy-smitten, and would never move again— never again speak to her! At this terrible thought, Alice left her seat, and drew nearer to that sad and silent figure. She laid her own hand upon the cold hand which rested on the table; it did not move to meet the proffered clasp.

"Oh, grandmother! dear grandmother!" burst from the girl's lips in sudden penitence; "forgive me—oh, do forgive me! I have been too unmindful of your love and care; can you forgive me? I have been very wrong."

Not a word, not a motion betrayed that she had been heard; and, wild with terror, she threw herself in quick, penitent tears at her grandmother's feet, and sobbed out her prayer to be forgiven.

Ah! it was her childhood's story over again. The doting grandmother could not hold out against the beloved penitent, and the loving arms unclosed to her once more. Again Alice was taken back in love and forgiveness, and again she wept out her passionate rebellion upon that true and faithful heart.

Ah, happy for them both that the reconciliation was not deferred until it was too late—that they "suffered not the sun to go down upon their wrath;" that with tender, loving words and fond embraces and murmured blessings they parted for the night.

CHAPTER XVII.

IN DANGER.

"Send down thy bright-winged angel, Lord !
Amid the night so wild ;
And bid him come and breathe upon,
And heal our gentle child."

GAIN darkness spread its shadowy wings over the little dwelling of Mistress Campbell, and its inmates separated ; but again poor Alice passed a restless and feverish night, tossing and turning in painful sleeplessness, wearied and exhausted in mind and body, but still seemingly condemned to sad watchfulness.

It might have been something peculiar in the heavy atmosphere which oppressed her, for the sultry night air was surcharged with electricity ; or it might have been merely the natural result of the overtasking of nerve and brain which the sensitive girl had undergone during the last two days; but sleep seemed denied her.

Oh! how welcome to her would have been only one short hour of that calm, dreamless slumber, light as the sleep of infancy, which she had never learned to appreciate till the lesson came to her through its loss. Oh! for only one short hour of blessed sleep, to calm her wild, feverish unrest—to take the sting of pain out of the hot and dazzled eyes, whose aching lids seemed as if they would never again close over the strained vision.

In vain. She lay, restlessly tossing and moaning—only made conscious of a momentary drowse, when a sudden nervous start betrayed to her that she had been treading the border-lands of sleep. Yet it was not so much the sad memories of the past, or the doubts, hopes, and anxieties of the future, which dwelt now upon her mind, and kept her waking, as it had been the night before. Her mind was perhaps quite as much and as unnaturally overtasked; but it was far less clear, and its condition was wholly different.

On the preceding night, although painfully excited and disturbed, the action of her mind had still been coherent and natural—the objects which had then passed in review before her were real, though distressing, and she had mind and memory enough to think them out, and follow them up to their legitimate conclusion; but now it was the delirium of coming fever—her mind drifted beyond her control, and her brain was filled with the rapidly shifting, weird, and often grotesque visions of an incoherent and disordered imagination.

A strange physical drowsiness, that was not sleep, contended with a fierce mental activity that was not wakefulness; and she lay, vaguely watching the procession of fantastic figures which moved around her, wondering if they could be real, yet wholly unable to convince herself that they were false; now feebly laughing at their mocking show—then cowering from them in weak terror.

Slowly—slowly, the heavy hours of the night crept by; and was it wonderful if, when the tardy morning broke at last, she was wholly unable to rise—unable to lift her weary, aching head from its heated pillow —and that her grandmother found her with burning cheeks, rapid pulse, throbbing temples, and all the terrible premonitory symptoms of fever?

But Elsie Campbell, who was an experienced and tender nurse, though fully aware of the danger which threatened her darling, met it with calm demeanor and active remedies. With her loving heart wrung to its very core, she wasted no time in idle questions or useless protestations; her loving, active hands shut out the light from the sad, staring eyes—tenderly bound the moistened linen round the tortured brow—bathed the burning cheeks, and held the cooling drink to the parched and thirsting lips. She fanned the languid sufferer, lifted the feeble form to an easier position, or held the aching head upon her kind, maternal bosom.

It seemed as if all memory of their recent feud had passed from the mind of each—all was forgiven and forgotten. Alice, moaning and tossing, with the unconscious selfishness which sickness so often awakens in the inexperienced in suffering, calling freely for all her grandmother's tender care and loving sympathy, forgot she had so lately doubted them; and poor Elsie, hanging over her in soothing ministrations, with a perpetual prayer in her heart, remembered only her darling's present danger, and forgot she had ever been less than dutiful.

Mistress Campbell was well skilled in all the homely curative lore upon which, in the olden days, experience relied. She knew the health-giving properties hidden in herbs and roots and barks—the simple remedies drawn from Nature's own laboratory—and which, if possibly less potent for good, were far more harmless than the drugs of our modern pharmacists; and so, through the long, uncounted hours of the bright, hot summer's day—through the slow-moving watches of the sultry summer night—the patient watcher kept her weary place by the sick-bed, with tireless ministry, and tender, soothing words; and by her skill and love seemed to hold even the "king of terrors" at bay, and actually to ward off the impending danger. It was a fearful contest, for life or death, and often poor Mistress Campbell's heart sank within her; but as the second day drew toward its close, her experienced eye detected a hopeful though very gradual change.

The burning fever was lessened; the torturing pain in the temples was subdued; the restlessly tossing limbs relaxed their painful tension, and sunk into easier attitudes of rest; the rapid pulse grew slower and more regular; the quick, gasping respiration became deeper and less rapid; a gentle moisture broke out on the parched skin, and Alice dozed off into a light and broken slumber beneath the glad eye of the watcher, who held her breath to listen with thankful heart, as the health-bringing sleep grew more and more profound, until, as the cooler shades of night came on, the young sufferer lay in calm and peaceful rest, beneath the glad eyes that ventured now to weep in very thankfulness.

Deeper and deeper grew that blessed, saving slumber as the night wore on, only broken when Alice was aroused to take the offered medicine or nourishment, which she received with grateful consciousness, and then sank back to quiet sleep again; and still the grandmother watched and waited, with a perpetual song of thanksgiving at her heart.

It was late in the morning of the third day when Alice awoke from her restorative sleep, calm and refreshed, and with a clear brain; but weak—oh! weak—to almost infantine weakness. Instinctively she turned her head to address her faithful watcher; but she missed the dear old familiar face, which she remembered had bent like that of a guardian angel above her. But with returning clearness of mind had come back Alice's habitual thoughtfulness for the comfort of others; and remembering her grandmother's patient and protracted watching, she naturally concluded she had left her to seek the refreshment of needed sleep, and she kept very quiet, resolved not to disturb her, but to wait patiently until she came to her.

But she waited long and vainly—no one came; and at last, feeling the need of nourishment, and hearing Winny moving with restless steps in the room below, she called to her, faintly at first, for fear of disturbing her grandmother; but as her call seemed unheard or unheeded, she raised herself painfully from her pillow and called again.

And Winny came — but oh! merciful heavens! what had happened? What was the awful horror that spoke in those great, wildly rolling eyes—which had blanched to a gray ashiness that dusky face?

"Oh! Winny, Winny, what is it? Oh! tell me — tell me at once," murmured the girl's pale, quivering lips—"tell me what it is. I can bear any thing better than silence. Tell me—oh! tell me—or I shall go mad."

And poor Winny, thus adjured, did tell. She had been cautioned not to tell—to wait, and let others break the sad tidings carefully to Alice; but grief and horror rendered all precaution impossible to her, as, throwing herself down in abject terror, she burst out with the terrible truth in all the passionate volubility of her race.

Goody Campbell had been cried out upon by the accusing girls—the constables had come with a warrant that morning and taken her away to jail, to be tried as a witch, like poor Goody Nurse!

And Alice heard and comprehended it all —and then, shrieking in wild delirium, she sunk back upon her bed in utter unconsciousness, and knew no more.

CHAPTER XVIII.

MISTRESS CAMPBELL'S TRIAL.

"Perchance Elijah thought his fate was sealed—
That God had sent premonitory warning;
And that the croaking ravens but revealed
His death to-morrow morning."

WHEN poor Mistress Campbell, dizzy with want of sleep, and worn and weary with her anxious and long-protracted watch, was summoned from her grandchild's sick-bed, in the chill gray of the early morning, to encounter the stern messengers of the law, her first instinctive thought was the fear that Alice might be disturbed.

Of her own impending danger she took not the slightest heed—indeed, she scarcely realized it; for, conscious of her own entire innocence of the crime imputed to her, and ignorant that she had any enemies or ill-wishers, she never doubted that the whole thing was a mistake, and that it needed only to be explained to be rectified at once; and she confidently made this assertion. But in answer to this, the officers produced the warrant for her arrest, in which her name was plainly inserted.

Still, though surprised and indignant at the ignominy and shame which such a charge, even if unfounded, must leave upon her hitherto spotless good name in the little community, she felt no personal fear for the result. Her only thought was for Alice — Alice, sick and in danger. How could she leave her, when perhaps that precious life — so much dearer than her own — yet hung upon her continued care? — and with tears and entreaties that she would have scorned to use in her own behalf, she pleaded earnestly for a short delay.

She told the officials of the dangerous nature of her grandchild's illness, and tried to touch their feelings. She promised, with solemn protestations, that she would not leave the house, but would consider herself their prisoner — and wait, and be found there, ready to answer any future legal summons, if they would only leave her for a few days to watch over her sick child. But she pleaded in vain; her words fell upon unheeding ears. Possibly the men had, by virtue of their office, become inured to such scenes, and their hearts were hardened to them; or it might be that the very imputation of being a witch had shut her off from all human sympathy; but the officials were deaf to her tearful pleading, inexorable in the performance of their cruel duties, and would admit of no delay.

Still, even then, amid all the agitation of that hurried and terrible home-leaving, with true motherly love, the afflicted woman thought only of Alice, and contrived to send a message to her friends at Nurse's Farm to inform them of her own arrest and Alice's illness, and asking them to come, and comfort and care for her darling in her own enforced absence from her home.

And these sisters in affliction answered the appeal at once, and hastened to Alice's bedside — though not, as we have seen, in time to prevent the terrible disclosure which poor terrified Winny had made.

But it would have made, possibly, but little difference in fact how the terrible story was told. No cautious words, however carefully chosen—no tender, pitying tones, however sympathetic—could have robbed that awful communication of its fearful meaning. But they found poor Alice wildly raving in a relapse of the fever which her grandmother's devotion and skill had so nearly averted, and they took charge of the desolate household, and watched over the suffering girl with sisterly love.

But while Alice, blessed by her very unconsciousness, lay battling with the fierce fever which had fastened upon her, and tended by the loving care of the few true and faithful friends whom misfortune and danger only drew more closely to her side, her grandmother's free and active spirit chafed in her close confinement within the narrow limits of the jail.

The clever, bustling, active housekeeper, who had kept herself busy with all the details of her little household, and to whom fresh air and active out-of-door exercise seemed to be a very necessity of her being, was helpless and cramped in chains and bondage; she, to whom "cleanliness was next to godliness," was sickened and disgusted by the dirt and discomfort all around her; and far more than all these lesser evils was the heart's deep craving for the companionship of her child, from whom until now she had never been separated for a single night since Alice's infancy; and now this one treasure of her otherwise desolate heart was ill—possibly dying—and she was kept from her.

This thought exasperated her beyond measure. Her knowledge of her own entire innocence made the unfounded charge seem almost an absurdity in her eyes. She could not realize that others, from a different standpoint, took different views; and she felt a thorough contempt for what seemed to her the willful blindness of her accusers and prosecutors, and this sentiment she did not hesitate openly to declare.

It was strange that her reliance upon her own innocence should have rendered her thus fearless, with the tragic fate of poor Goody Nurse before her, for she believed in her friend's integrity as fully as in her own.

But then it must be remembered that Rebecca Nurse had made many personal enemies by the part she had taken in the former Church controversy, and to their malicious revenge many persons attributed her condemnation; while she herself was wholly uncompromised in these matters, and was not aware of an enemy.

At length, when worn with her confinement and irritated with delay, she was arraigned for trial, and the same formulas were gone through with that had marked the trials of her unfortunate predecessors; but Elsie Campbell, with her heart full of anxiety for her child, and bitter contempt and hatred of her judges, was a sharp match for the sharpest of her opponents.

Reckless of all possible consequences — fearless by nature — sure that a trial must make her innocence clear to all — and stung to madness by the uncalled-for malice of her accusers and the injustice of her confinement, her sharp Scottish shrewdness and quick mother wit flashed back upon them in angry, scornful words.

When she was placed at the bar, Justice

Hathorne (who seems to have combined in his own single person the several duties of judge and prosecuting officer, in a manner that is incomprehensible to our modern ideas of legal etiquette) thus addressed her:

"Elsie Campbell, look at me. You are now in the hands of authority; answer, then, with truth."

"I kinna answer ye wi' ony ither. The truth is my mither tongue—I aye speak it."

"Tell me, then, why do you torment these children?"

"I dinna torment them. I niver hurted a bairn in my life—I'd scorn to do it."

"But they say that you do."

"I kinna help wha' they say. I am jist an honest, God-fearin' woman; I dinna ken aught o' yer witchcraft."

"But what, then, makes them say it of you?"

"Hoo suld I ken? I kinna fash mysel' to tell hoo ilka fule's tongue may wag."

"But do you not know that if you are guilty you can not hide it?"

"Haith! an' I ken that weel enow; an' sae do the Lord abune us."

"Yea, He doth; and He hath power to discover the guilty, and bring them to open shame."

"In varry deed He hath. He kin gie wisdom to the simple — may he open the een o' magistrates an' ministers."

"Do you think to find mercy by denying and aggravating your sin?"

"Alas! that is a true word—na', I dinna think it."

"You should look for it, then, in God's way."

"An' sae I do; an' in nae ither."

"Here are three or four witnesses who testify against you."

"Weel-a-weel, an' what kin I do? Many may rise up again' me—I kinna help it. If a' be again' me, what can I do?"

"You said just now that we magistrates needed to have our eyes opened."

"Did I say that? Na'—na', I but said I prayed it might be."

"Do you mean to say that we are blind, then?"

"I suld think ye maun be, if ye kin see a witch in me."

"I hear you have said that you would open our eyes for us."

"Na'—na', I ne'er said the word; I wad na' be that presumptuous."

"What do you mean by that?"

"That I think it is far abune me. It wad tak' the power o' Him who opened blind Bartimeus his eyes."

This allusion to the supposed professional blindness of the court which the prisoner at the bar was accused of having made, seems to have rankled in the breast of Justice Hathorne with peculiar bitterness; and her spirited answer, although it might silence, was certainly not calculated to conciliate him—indeed, the whole conduct and bearing of the prisoner, both in confinement and upon trial, was rasping and irritating in the extreme, and such as to increase the prejudice already existing against her.

But it must be remembered in her extenuation that, believing the charge brought against her had originated in some absurd ignorance, which would be brought to light in the course of events, and would triumphantly vindicate her good name, she could not believe that even her persecutors really believed in it; and exasperated at what she considered an unauthorized and unlawful interference in her private rights, in compelling her to leave her home and the bedside of her sick child, she assumed a defiant and even contemptuous attitude, to which the sharpness of her foreign tongue gave perhaps additional point.

But Justice Hathorne continued his investigations, which seem to have had little method:

"You may have engaged not to confess your sins."

"I wa' na' brought up to make confessions to men—I am nae papist."

"But God knoweth the heart."

"So he doth—that is a true word, an' I confess my sins to him."

"And who is your God?"

"Surely, the God who made me."

"What is his name?"

"The Lord God Almighty; glory be to his holy name; an' may he keep his servants in the hour o' their trial."

"Hath he no other name?"

“ Yes, he is sometimes called ‘ the Lord Jehovah.’ ”

“ And does the one you pray to tell you *he* is God ?”

“ I dinna pray to ony but the God that made me.”

“ Do you not believe there are witches in the country ?”

“ Sure, I dinna ken there is ony; I am but a stranger an’ sojourner here—what do I ken ?”

“ Why do you laugh ?”

“ Did I laugh? I did na’ ken it; but weel I may at sich folly.”

“ I ask you—what ails these people ?”

“ I dinna ken; how suld I, when they are strangers to me ?”

“ But they say that you have tormented them.”

“ An’ I say it is na’ true. Why suld I ? I hae nae ill-will to them, I dinna ken aee-thing aboot them.”

“ But if not—what do you think ails them ?”

“ I dinna ken—an’ I dinna desire to spend my sma’ judgment upon it.”

"But do you think they are bewitched?"

"Na'; I dinna think they are."

"Well, then—what do you think about them?"

"I kinna say; my thoughts are my ain whiles I keep them to mysel'; but ance they are out, they are anither's."

"But who do you think is their master?"

"That is nae affair o' mine—I dinna serve him."

"But who do you think they serve?"

"Aiblins they be dealin' in the black art, ye maun ken as weel as I."

"Do you believe they do not speak the truth?"

"'Deed; an' they may lee, for a' I ken."

"And why may not you lie as well?"

"I dare na' tell a lee—not if it wad save my life."

"Pray God discover you, if you are guilty," said the examiner impatiently; and the dauntless woman responded fervently, "Amen! amen! so be it; but a fause tongue can ne'er make an innocent bodie guilty."

Up to this time, this rather pointless ex-

amination had failed to prove any thing; and
now the accusers, seeing doubtless that the
popular sympathy was on the side of the
spirited old woman, and that the case was
evidently going against them, fell into dreadful convulsions, and writhed in strong contortions, giving utterance to fearful groans
and shrieks.   When this disturbance was
over, and quiet was again restored, the magistrate asked the prisoner: "Is it possible
that you have no pity for these afflicted
ones?" and she calmly replied, "Na'; I hae
nae pity to waste on them."

"Do you not feel that God is discovering
you?"

"Ne'er a bit; but if ye kin prove me
guilty, I maun lie under it."

At last, after a consultation, the magistrate
informed her that one of her accusers had
testified that she had been known to torture
and cruelly use the young maid, her own
grandchild, living with her.

"Alas! that she is na' to the fore to speak
for me," said poor Elsie; "*she* wad na' say
sae; but she is lyin' deein' at hame, her
lane, puir lambie."   And at the thought of her

darling's danger, thus suddenly brought before her, tears, that her own woes had not called forth, fell thick and fast upon her fettered hands.

The wily accuser saw her advantage, and hastened to press it on.

"She has said so—she has been heard to say it, and you yourself have heard her."

"She ha' said it—said what?" said Elsie, starting like a war-horse at the sound of the trumpet. "What ha' she said?"

"That you were cruel to her; that you had no mercy; that you stabbed her to the heart and tortured her."

As these terrible words fell upon her ears, a burning flush rose to poor Mistress Campbell's brow; too well she remembered Alice's passionate and heedless words—too clearly she realized now who had been listening beneath her window on that sad night; and as the utter impossibility of ever clearing herself from this new and horrible imputation broke upon her, she wrung her fettered hands in anguish, sank back and groaned aloud.

Of course the impression this made was

overwhelming: it was regarded as a clear and signal proof of her guilt. There was a momentary silence, and then the justice spoke again:

"Did I not say truly that God was discovering you? What will you say to this?"

"That it is fause," said Goody Campbell, starting up; "it is as fause as the leein' lips that say it."

"Do you deny the truth of it, then? Can you say that your grandchild never said it?"

"Na'!" said the unhappy prisoner, trembling with wrath and shame, "I'll na' deny it; but they were thoughtless, heedless words, if the lassie did utter them, and had naught to do wi' witchcraft."

"How did the maid happen to use them, then?"

"She did na' mean them; I wa' tellin' the lassie somewhat that happened at hame, years agone, afore iver she wa' born, when she said it."

"And what was the strange event which, happening so long ago, called out so much feeling? You will please state it to the court."

"It wa' somewhat wi' which the coort ha' nathing to do," persisted Elsie, who would have died sooner than tell the story of her daughter's wrong in open court. "It wa' jist an auld world story, an' I am na' free to tell it here."

Insinuation, question, and cross-examination failed to draw any thing more from the wary and determined old woman, and she was remanded to jail.

Of course the impression she had made was a very unfavorable one; her sharpness had irritated her judges, and the pertinacity with which she refused to gratify the curiosity of the court was looked upon as a sure test of her guilt.

Twice more she was arraigned, and still she refused to give any further explanation of the ominous words; and her refusal to comply being regarded as contumacy and contempt of court, in addition to the primary charge against her, the verdict of the jury was "Guilty"—and she was condemned and sentenced to death.

And Alice, raving in the delirium of fever, was spared the agony of knowing that her passionate words, caught up by revenge and repeated by malice, forged the terrible link in the chain of evidence which condemned her grandmother to a felon's death.

CHAPTER XIX.

WAITING FOR DEATH.

"How much the heart may bear, and yet not break!
    How much the flesh may suffer, and not die!
I question much if any pain or ache,
    Of soul or body, brings our end more nigh.
Though we are sick, and tired, and faint, and worn—
    Lo! all things can be borne."

ND poor Alice lay ill for weeks, hovering long between life and death, and all unconscious of the bitter woe that was awaiting her tardy recovery——a woe so vast that even her loving attendants, having had to pass through the same terrible experience themselves, almost hoped she might never awaken to the consciousness of it, but find her grandmother in a better world, without the agony of the parting in this.

But youth is strong, and Alice had a good constitution, and she rallied at last; but oh!

to what a bitter awakening!—to find her nearest and dearest, her only known relative, languishing in chains and bondage, and under condemnation to death.

But it was worse than useless to attempt to keep the awful truth from her—it must be made known; and Alice—the petted child, the creature hitherto of the sunshine and the summer—had to listen to the communication which must strike the summer and the sunshine out of all her future life.

But the moment she was able to stand alone she insisted upon going at once to her grandmother; and dreadful as their meeting must be, her friends felt there was nothing to be gained by delaying it; while Alice felt as if every moment of that doomed life was far too precious to her to be wasted apart; and soon the morning, noon, and evening found the faithful child feebly creeping, with weak, tottering steps, back and forth, to and from the miserable prison, where her presence brought the only ray of comfort that could enter those melancholy walls; and even the hardened jailers grew to know and pity the beautiful and desolate young creature, and opened their doors to her, when they refused admittance to others.

But though Alice's presence gave comfort to the weary prisoner, the grandmother was the one to essay the part of comforter. By a strong effort of her indomitable will, she had reconciled herself to her fate. She knew she was to suffer unjustly; but surely, she argued, it was far better so than if she had merited her sentence. Death, early or late, was the natural finale of every life, and what did a few more years of old age and infirmity have to offer her?

The one great trouble upon her mind was the thought of Alice's future. Alone in the world—beautiful, friendless, and penniless (for she well knew that by her attainder as a witch all her little property would be confiscated)—what was to become of her? Only the "Father of the fatherless" could know; and often, lifting her poor manacled hands to heaven, she prayed for his mercy and guardianship for her desolate child.

It was a striking but not unnatural proof of the unselfish love of the parent and child, that while the former, setting aside all question of her own forfeited life, dwelt ever upon the future life of her darling, vainly striving to form some idea of what her existence would be after her own was ended, Alice's thoughts never wandered beyond that terrible event—*that* was to her the termination of all things. To her the world itself would end with the life of her only relative. After *that*, all was a blank to her. Up to that terrible hour, all was blind agony and useless prayer, and then—"after *that*—the deluge."

And so, while Mistress Campbell wasted away in prison, the dreadful day was fast approaching, and no voice was raised to plead for her, no hand was lifted to avert her terrible doom.

How, indeed, could there be, when Alice's warmest, steadiest, and most powerful friends were the various members of the Nurse family? They had tried, as we have seen, every expedient in their own case: by appeals to justice and clemency; by certificates and testimonials; by fervent entreaties for delay and a new trial; and they had all signally failed. They knew, and felt it was worse than useless to attempt it again in behalf of another; and thus, while they surrounded Alice with their loving attentions, and comforted and supported her by every means in their power, they regarded it as only cruelty to encourage in her hopes which they felt a sure conviction must only end in disappointment.

One day, when Alice was searching at their desolate home for some article which her grandmother required, she chanced to come quite unexpectedly upon the little wampum chain which Pashemet had given her at their last parting; and as she lifted the simple pledge of friendship in her trembling hands, and thought of the kind words then spoken by him, her tears fell freely over it. The peaceful scene when it had been bestowed upon her—the quiet water, the overhanging trees, the mellow sunset—all rose upon her memory in strong contrast with the fearful present. Could it be indeed the same world? That happy, untroubled security! It was so short a time ago, in reality, and yet, in the momentous events which had crowded into it, it seemed like a period of long years.

"Oh, Pashemet, Pashemet! my brother!"

she murmured, in a voice broken by her sobs; "he little knows how wretched I am now. Ah! he would help me if he could—he said he would; but alas! alas! he can not help me—no one can help me now."

But Alice's friends were far too few to suffer her to forget one of them; and although she was sure Pashemet could not aid her, still she felt as if even the knowledge of his true, though distant, sympathy and sorrow for her in her dreadful affliction, if ineffectual, would yet be soothing to her lonely heart. So giving the little token into the hands of the faithful old Winny, she directed her to send it to Pashemet by the hands of an old neighbor, who belonged to the Naumkeag tribe of Indians, and tell him of her great distress, and of her grandmother's dreadful fate.

How and what was the Indian method of conveying tidings, secretly and speedily, through the intervening wilds and unbroken forests of a then uninhabited country, has, we believe, never yet been satisfactorily explained. We know that they were fleet of foot, and of untiring strength in the race; but whether information was thus posted on from hand to hand, as was wont to be done by the Scottish clansmen in the days of old, we know not; but it is a well-authenticated fact that intelligence was conveyed among them with marvelous speed and unerring certainty: and Alice felt sure the little token and the message would reach her friend, although she hoped and expected nothing more from it than his deep, brotherly interest in her sad misfortune; but to her, who stood so much alone in the world, even to feel that there existed for her this one little bond of sympathy with a true and loving heart was a relief.

CHAPTER XX.

THE DAY OF EXECUTION.

"Perhaps the dreaded future has less bitterness than I think—
The Lord may sweeten the water before I stoop to drink—
Or, if Marah must be Marah, He will stand beside the brink."

TIME, the inexorable messenger, whose tardy pace no passionate wishes, however ardent, can accelerate, whose rapid flight no breaking heart can arrest, moving on in his regular course, all unheeding of human joys and sorrows—ever the same, regardless "if empires rise or empires fall"—was bringing on the dreadful hour.

The last terrible day—the day appointed for the execution—had come. Clear, bright, and beautiful it dawned upon the earth, as if its cloudless light was sent in mockery, to tantalize the sad eyes which were doomed before it reached its zenith to be closed in death, and see its sweet light no more forever.

The unhappy prisoner, who though worn and pallid with the rigorous confinement, which told fearfully upon her active nature, used to sun and air and unlimited liberty of motion, had borne it uncomplainingly, had made but one request—and that, alas ! could not be complied with. She had prayed that Alice might be kept away from her on that last solemn occasion. She had felt when she parted from her darling the night before, with mingling tears, blessings, and caresses, and sent her from her, that the worst of death was over, and she begged that that bitter agony might not be renewed.

But Alice would not be thus kept away. She counted as a miser does his treasure every moment that remained to her of that precious life, although she, too, well knew that every moment was a renewed anguish. She could not be kept back except by actual violence, and that no one had the authority or the heart to use. She was early at the prison doors, and would be admitted. But over those last sad moments we must drop the veil of silence—they are too sacred for words.

"There is a tear for all who die, a mourner o'er the humblest grave;"—for death is always death; no lavished words, no mitigating circumstances can make it any thing *less*—but do we never think how aggravating circumstances may make it *more?*

We weep when we stand by the death-bed of our beloved ones, and watch the fading eye, and fondly clasp the nerveless hand; they may have been spared to us even to the utmost limitation of human life, and yet our affections can not let them go. Death comes to them, as our hearts know and our lips acknowledge, from the hand of a loving Father, sent perhaps as a welcome release from tears and pains, from weakness and infirmity—but yet *it is death*, and our hearts rebel against it. We may have been permitted to watch over them in loving tenderness; we have surrounded them with all that love or skill or science could devise for their relief; we have walked with them hand in hand, and smoothed and cheered their path through "the dark valley," and yet, "when the long parting summons them away," it is *death*—still *death;* and our wounded hearts cry out, and refuse to be comforted.

But what do we know of the agony of those who see the impending blow coming, not from the beneficent and all-wise Father, whose right to the creature he has made we do not dispute, but from man, the petty instrument of a fallible judgment, stepping in between the Creator and the created? Who see the beloved one moving before them, in fullness of health, in unimpaired vigor of mind and body, and in undoubted love and faith, and yet know that before another sun shall set that precious life shall be crushed out by brute violence?

"Heaven in its mercy hides the book of fate"—but man, unpitying man, sets the inevitable hour full before his victim's eye, and the terrible moments melt away, each one bearing off a visible portion of the life still palpitating in the heart.

Ah! we say such agony is too great to be borne. But it has been borne by hearts as tender and as loving as our own.

And how can human nature endure it? We know not—we only know that it has been borne. "Lo! all things can be borne." And it was this bitterest portion that poor Alice was called upon to suffer.

The last terrible moment had come. The sun had climbed to the mid-heaven, as if to look down upon the sacrifice, when the door of the prison was opened, and the unhappy prisoner came forth—not led forth, for the brave and dauntless old woman came out unsupported, and walking with a firm, un-faltering step.

There was a marked and striking differ-ence between Goody Nurse and Mistress Elsie Campbell. Both went to their death unflinchingly; but one had the meek resig-nation of a humble Christian, the other the fierce heroism of a Stoic: the first was saint-ly, the last was majestic.

Conscious of her own integrity, and of the falsity of the malicious charges against her, and full, as we have seen, of unmitigated contempt for the tribunal before which she had been so unjustly condemned, the spirit of the old Scottish Covenanters was roused within her. Her face, though perfectly col-orless, was set as a flint; and, like the Indian warrior at the stake, she was fixed in her purpose that no trembling nerve, no faltering step, should gratify the malice of her enemies by a token of her suffering.

So she came out, disdaining support, and would have mounted the fatal cart unaided, had not her manacled limbs forbidden it.

When she was placed in the vehicle, another vain attempt was made by Alice's friends to withdraw her from the awful scene; but the faithful child would not be removed. With wild eyes and piteous hands she waved them back. Twice she essayed to speak, but the unuttered words died on her feverish lips. Again — and they who stood nearest to her caught only the words, "Having loved his own, He *loved them to the end;*" and awed and silent, they desisted, and made way for her.

Clinging tightly with both her clenched hands to the back of the cart, to support her tottering and uncertain steps, with her uncovered head bent down upon her hands, and her bright, disheveled hair falling as a veil about her, Alice followed as the melancholy procession moved onward — up the length of Prison Lane (now St. Peter's Street) into Essex Street.

As the gloomy train wound along its way through the crowd, and just as it turned the corner into Essex Street, an Indian, closely wrapped in his blanket, dropped, as if by the merest chance, a bit of pine-bough into the slow-moving cart.

Apparently by accident the little missile fell; but it had been thrown by a dexterous hand, and with a calculated and certain aim. Lightly it brushed Alice's fair, bended head, touched her clenched hands, and fell into the cart before her. But Alice, moving on in a trance of giddy horror, with her heart "so full that feeling almost seemed unfelt," did not notice it. If she had, she might have recognized in it a token of the hope it was meant to convey to her.

Pashemet had received the little wampum chain—he was true to his pledge. Even then he was in town with a party of his bravest young warriors, although to make himself known even to Alice would possibly have defeated his object.

Gradually and unobserved, half a dozen

Indians, closely wrapped in their blankets, had mingled in the crowd—their stolid, inscrutable faces expressing neither interest nor sympathy in the sad scene passing before them. But under those blankets they were fully armed; under those dark, inexpressive faces there was keenest observation and intent purpose; and in a little wooded hollow, near the fatal " Gallow's Hill," a dozen or more fleet little shaggy Indian ponies were quietly picketed, waiting for their fierce, tameless riders.

The plan was perfected in its most minute details. The town officials, unsuspicious of opposition, were unarmed. The surprise was to take place at the moment of transit from the cart to the ladder. All was in readiness, and the rescue would undoubtedly have been successfully made had not circumstances wholly unlooked for chanced to prevent it.

The street was crowded with spectators, as upon the former executions; but it was clearly evident there was a change of sentiment in the lookers-on. Possibly the thirst for blood had now been satiated, and had died out—the tide of popular feeling was evidently turning. The faith in the accusers, once so unquestioning, had been lessened: the girls had become too confident and too reckless. Or it might be that possibly a new-born pity was awakened in behalf of the victims; and who could wonder?

In a small community, such as Salem then was, the private history, the affairs and personalities of each of its inhabitants is considered as the joint property of all the rest; consequently Alice's desolate orphan girlhood—her entire dependence upon the condemned prisoner, who was her only known relative in the wide world, might have well awakened pity under any circumstances; but, beyond this, the rare beauty of the poor girl, her sweet innocence, and her fearless devotion to her grandmother, had called forth the interest and admiration of many who had never personally known her; and now, instead of the coarse jeers, curses, and bitter invectives with which the howling mob had followed the first sufferers, there was, as they passed along, an awed and respectful silence —broken only now and then by sobs and sighs, and half-uttered exclamations of "God help them."

As the sad procession wound its slow way beneath the scorching noonday sun, toiling up the little crooked, narrow street, an interruption occurred. In one of the very narrowest portions of the street a gay cavalcade was seen approaching—their gay military harness ringing out and glittering in the sunbeams.

It was the new governor, Sir William Phips, who had only arrived in the country in the previous May; and who was now riding into town, accompanied by a party of officers, most of them composing his suite, and one or two personal friends.

Laughing and jesting in true military style, they drew near; but the street was too narrow to allow of two such pageants at one time, and for once grim Death stood back, jostled out of the way by busy, joyful Life.

The miserable, creaking, jolting death-cart drew up on one side of the narrow street, and halted, to allow the governor and his suite to pass by.

At the sudden stoppage of the cart, poor Alice started from her ghastly drowse—possibly she thought the terrible goal was reached. As she lifted her head and looked wildly around with her sad, frightened, bewildered eyes, the words which were passing from lip to lip around her fell upon her ear: "It is his Excellency, Sir William Phips, the new governor."

In one instant, straight and clear as a flash of light from heaven, broke in upon her clouded mind an intuitive ray of hope; in one moment she had quitted the cart to which she had convulsively clung, and with one wild bound, like the death-leap of some maddened creature, she sprung directly in Sir William's path, and flinging up her wild arms to arrest him, she raised her sad, beseeching eyes to his, and faltered out her impassioned appeal: "Mercy! mercy! your Excellency; pardon—pardon—for the sweet love of heaven—*she is innocent!* Oh! as you hope for mercy in your own sorest need hereafter, have mercy upon us — mercy! mercy!"

As the frantic creature paused for breath,

she sank exhausted upon the ground just in front of the governor's horse; and startled by the sudden apparition of the fair, spirit-like thing, Sir William sat in silent bewilderment, reining in his plunging, snorting horse with a powerful hand, till the spirited animal sank upon his haunches beneath the strong control.

But Sir William's were not the only eyes to which that fair, frantic face appealed: one of the officers in the company, who had come out from England with the governor, galloped to the scene, and forcing his horse up to the side of the death-cart, peered with quick, inquiring eyes into the face of the prisoner, who had sat with closed eyes and tightly compressed lips, not turning her head or moving hand or foot since she entered that car of death; then suddenly, as if his gaze had assured him of her identity, he bent forward and shouted close to her ear, "Elsie Campbell!—look at me!"

With a mighty effort, the fast-sealed eyes unclosed; and the thoughts which had, it would seem, already preceded her to the unknown and eternal world she was so soon to enter, turned back once more to earth; she did not speak, but her involuntary start, and the sudden rush of color that flushed her pallid face, betrayed her recognition of him.

Grasping her firmly by the arm, he asked in breathless entreaty: "Tell me—who is that girl? I adjure you—by the memory of Alice—answer me."

For one moment Elsie Campbell wavered —here was the betrayer of her only child— and for one moment revenge seemed sweet to her still; but then she thought of Alice, her darling, left alone in the wide, cruel world—no friend, no protector; this man was her father—and love conquered pride: the rigid lips painfully unclosed, and with an evident effort she murmured hoarsely: "Your child, my lord!—my Alice's daughter."

Another moment, and the officer had sprung from his saddle and stood by Sir William's side, his eager hand upon the governor's arm.

"Sir William—hear me; you know my life's sad history, and my unsuccessful search; I believe that girl to be my long-sought child; that woman is the mother of my sainted wife—she is the sole possessor of the coveted secret; I will answer for her innocence of this absurd charge. I ask you, by our life-long friendship, to use in her behalf the executive clemency which you hold."

The hands of the brother officers met in a wringing clasp; and then, while the father pressed forward and raised the unconscious form of Alice from the ground, there was a sudden stir and conference among the officers of the governor's council, a few words to his secretary, a few hasty formulas—and then. the magic words, " A reprieve—a reprieve! pardon — pardon ! the governor's pardon !" were caught up by the nearest by-standers, and spread rapidly through the sympathizing crowd. The governor and his suite galloped onward; the clumsy, creaking deathcart was turned about, and followed them down to the "Ship Tavern," where Alice's father had already preceded them with his precious and unconscious burden; and here, when her swollen and long-manacled limbs were once more set at liberty, the trembling and half-bewildered grandmother assisted in recovering the still fainting and exhausted girl.

" Oh, tell me !" said the .father, who was supporting his child in his arms—looking up ·into Goody Campbell's face as she too bent over her darling—"Oh, tell me those blessed words again—tell me that this is indeed the child of my beloved Alice—my precious wife."

" An' wa' she your wife—in varry deed ?" asked the still doubting listener, with her keen, penetrating eyes fixed full upon his face.

" Was she my wife ? Good heavens ! yes —ten thousand times yes ! who dares to question it ? Yes ! my sainted Alice was my dear and honored wife ; did you—did any one ever doubt it ?"

" Yes," · said Elsie Campbell, meekly, " I did doot it—I wa' told it wa' a sham marriage, an' I believed it ; I thought you had done me an' my dead a mighty wrong, an' I could na' forgi'e it. But I see now that I hae done ye a mighty wrong, an' I dare na' ask ye to forgi'e me."

" I can forgive any thing to-day," said the

father, tremblingly, " if only this precious one, so long and so vainly sought, is spared to me ; but we have each of us much to explain."

And Alice was spared to them—but not till a long and dangerous illness had resulted from the unnatural strain of mind and body which the poor girl had undergone did they dare to hope ; and while hovering in united care and anxiety over their mutual treasure, the two watchers learned each other's mutual worth—and if they could never forget the heart sorrow they had each suffered and occasioned, at least they learned to forgive and respect.

CHAPTER XXI.

"It may be there was waiting for the coming of my feet,
Some gift of such rare blessedness, some joy so strangely sweet,
That my lips can only tremble with the thanks that I repeat."

BUT Alice was young and strong, and of an unbroken constitution; and youth, when aided by love and hope and happiness, recuperates rapidly. And the time soon came when Alice, sitting supported by her father's arms, with her trembling hand fondly clasped in that of her beloved grandmother, who seemed to her as one restored from the dead, could listen attentively to her father while he recounted to them the events of those passed years, which she had so longed to know and so vainly conjectured.

He described her mother to her as she was when they first met—her beauty, her purity, her loveliness; of his deep admiration of her; of the love she inspired in him from the first, and which he flattered himself she soon learned to reciprocate; and of his full and fixed determination to win her for his wife.

Then he told her of the obstacles which his father's more mercenary views for the greater aggrandizement of him, as his only son, had thrown in his way; and that the marriage which his father had so set his heart upon would have made his life wretched.

He explained to her that his father's disease, which was a softening of the brain, had been pronounced incurable, and that while he might live for years, any opposition would be sure to aggravate it; and that his medical attendants had plainly stated to him that to cross his wishes upon any point upon which they were strongly fixed would increase the difficulty under which he labored — would certainly be dangerous, and might prove fatal.

What, then, could he do? There was no hope of a favorable change in the future, and the postponement of his marriage might be prolonged for years. Under these circumstances he had persuaded Alice to consent to a private marriage; but this, though necessarily kept from the knowledge of his father, had been duly solemnized by his own clergyman, in the presence of his two uncles (who fully approved of it), and two or three other material witnesses.

He told her of his distress when his father concluded to go abroad for change of climate, and strenuously demanded he should accompany him, which he could not evade without declaring the fact of his marriage, which he dared not venture to do.

He told her of his deep grief and despair when in a foreign land he received the terrible tidings of his young wife's sudden death; of his heart-felt craving to know more; of the many letters which he had addressed to Mrs. Campbell, imploring her to give him the most minute details of all that related to his wife's sickness and death, but which had been all unanswered.

That when, by reason of his father's death, he had at last been free to return, he had hastened at once to Scotland to see her, but only to find all his letters still lying uncalled for at the post-office, and to learn that Mrs. Campbell, after the death of her daughter, had sold out all her possessions and departed, and no one could tell him where she had removed to. And he had only the melancholy satisfaction of having the beloved remains of his wife removed from their humble resting-place to the burial-place of his family, and a suitable monument erected to her memory as his wife.

That after the performance of this sacred duty he had prosecuted his search for Mrs. Campbell in every direction, hoping only to learn from her something of his wife's last hours; but in vain, until in a remote region of the Highlands he had come upon traces of her recent occupation of the little Hillside Farm.

Here he learned for the first time, to his infinite surprise, that she had with her a little girl of the same name as his wife, whom she called her granddaughter. As he well knew that she had not only no other child than his wife, but no other near relative, there arose in his mind the vague hope that Alice might have left a living child; and the description of the little girl's age and appearance confirmed this new hope. Yet, if so, why had the fact never been communicated to him? And his sole object and interest now in life was to find her. But Elsie Campbell had taken her measures too carefully, and concealed her trail too successfully for this.

For years he had prosecuted this eager but ever unsuccessful search, which had for him the only hope which life still held for him.

At last, baffled and worn out by repeated disappointments, he accepted the invitation of his friend Sir William Phips to try to forget his trouble in the excitement of visiting the New World, to which Sir William, in his new appointment of governor, was about to embark. In very hopelessness he consented to make the trial; and here, where he least expected it, and under circumstances stranger than fiction could invent, in the streets of Salem he found his long-sought child.

But even now the doting father felt he was not sure of the safety of his darling child, until he had her under the shelter of his own roof and the protection of his own country. He was eager to take her home; and as neither Alice nor her grandmother were reluctant to leave the land where they had suffered so much and had attained such an undesirable notoriety, preparations were made for their speedy departure for England so soon as Alice was able to bear the fatigue of the voyage.

But although it was fully decided that Grandmother Campbell was to cross the water with them, her own practical good sense showed her that she could not hope or expect to retain her place at her grandchild's side when Alice should assume her true position in her father's home; and it was her decided and openly declared intention to return to Scotland.

Alice, who, in spite of the pleadings of her own heart, saw the propriety of this step, strongly urged upon her a return to

the Hillside Farm, of which she still retained a very pleasant impression, as the
well-remembered and happy home of her
own childhood. But Mrs. Campbell did not
wish it. The six years they had passed
there, and which to the happy child, so petted and indulged, seemed in memory all
one unclouded day of enjoyment, had to
the grandmother been long years of the
most intense grief and constant anxiety, and
she had no pleasant associations with the
place.

The little Lowland farm, once occupied by
her parents, and which had been her own
patrimony, was now again, she had learned,
for sale. It was the scene of her own childhood and youth. It was consecrated to her
by the tender memories of her parents and
her only child. Here she was born. Its
kindly roof had given her a shelter when
she came back to it a deserted wife or desolate widow.

It was near enough to England to enable
her to see and hear from her beloved grandchild regularly; and the quiet grave-yard
where her parents slept was now to her the

dearest spot on earth. She would return there, to await the close of the eventful life which had there begun; and at her request an agent was authorized to make the purchase for her.

CHAPTER XXII.

THE PARTING.

"Sometimes beneath exterior rough
  A loyal soul is hidden,
That questions not the Master's will,
  But does the task that's bidden;
For lowly lot and form uncouth
  May yet perchance inherit
A grace the mighty Cæsar lacked—
  A calm, contented spirit."

THE person most aggrieved in the prospect of the departure of the little family was our humble friend, the faithful old Winny.

To her it was a loss to which nothing could reconcile her, and though (unlike herself) she bore it in silence, still it was plain to see that she drooped under it.

One day Alice found her sitting upon an inverted wash-tub in front of the hen-house, with her poor woolly head in her hands, in a very despondent attitude. Supposing she was grieving for her coming departure, Alice, who in the fullness of her own happiness longed to see every one else happy, said to her—

"Why, what is the matter, Winny? you seem to be in trouble. Tell me what it is, and see if I can not help you."

"So I be, ruther," said Winny, raising her dejected face; "but it aint nuffin' to trubble you wid. I wuz kinder 'flectin' like—dat's all."

"But I am afraid your reflections were sad ones," said Alice, kindly.

"Wal, dey wuz; I'm kinder puzzled like, Alice. Yer jest set down here, will yer?" and as she spoke she upset another of her tubs, dusted it, and, throwing her apron over it, signed to Alice to sit beside her; and Alice, who loved to humor the simple-hearted old woman, gravely complied, and sat *tête-à-tête* with her, prepared to listen.

"Yer see, Alice, de trubble is here. I'm feared I'se done wrong—kinder cheated like."

"Oh, no, Winny—no, indeed; I am sure you never cheated any one of a penny."

"Oh, no; it aint no money, an' I didn't mean to do nuffin' wrong; but I'm feared

I haz all de same, unbeknownst to me. Yer see, Alice, de care o' hens an' chickens is a mighty great 'sponsibility. Didn't yer neber tink so?"

"Why, no," said Alice, laughing, "I never have thought so; but still it may be—but how do you mean?"

"Well, dat are is what I'm goin' to tell yer. When dese 'ere hens dey fust begun to lay—little Speckle, she wuz the fust to be-gin, an' it wuz wery pretty o' her, an' I tort it wuz wery good manners.

"But yer see, little Speckle, she were a pert, forth-puttin', no-'count sort o' critter; an' her eggs—well, I s'pose she done her best—but her eggs, dey warn't nuffin' to speak ob—little tings, not much bigger dan a robin's eggs. So, as dey wasn't by no means fit to be sot, I jest used dem in de family as dey come along. But bime-by Brownie, she begun for to lay. Brownie is a real great, gen'rous sort o' hen, an' her eggs, dey wuz sum'pen like—big again as Speckle's wuz. I tell you dem wuz good measure, a credit to any hen, an' I kept dem to set.

"Ob course, Speckle, she habin' begun to lay fust, wuz de fust to want to set. She wuz allers a kinder forward young ting; an' as we wuz ompatient to hev some chickins, —an' I neber tort on't—I went an' sot her fust."

And here the speaker paused, and looked up at Alice, as if she had reached the point of the story.

"Well?" said Alice wonderingly, for she did not understand; "is she not doing well with the eggs, Winny?"

"Oh, lors, yes. She's a-doin' well enuff; but—"

"But what is the trouble, then? I do not see."

"Why, poor Brownie, ob course—don't yer see? Whose chicks will dey be, Alice?"

"Why Speckle's, of course," said Alice, "if she hatches them—won't they be?"

"Dere, dat's jest it; yes, I s'pose so. Dey'll be Speckle's chickins, an' dey didn't ought to be. Brownie, she laid dem eggs, an' now I've giv um to Speckle, an' I'll bet dat pert young ting she'll go a-troopin' round wid um, as proud as you please, right under Brownie's nose an' eyes; an' poor Brownie, she won't know dey're her'n; she'll tink dey are on'y her neffers an' nieces. Now aint dat are too bad? an' I done it!"

"Probably," said Alice, laughing at the old woman's troubled face, "Brownie will never find it out; and you know 'what the mind does not know the heart will not rue.' I guess she will stand it. But Winny, I want to ask about your father—how is old Drosky?"

"Oh, lors bress us! he's well enuff— strong as a horse, he is."

"I am glad to hear it. I have never seen him since the day he built this hen-coop."

"No, nor before eder. Don't yer remember how s'prised yer wuz to find I had dad? An' yer neber knowed yer had one yerself. I guess yer wuz more s'priseder yet when yer own come along. He is jest a beauty, your'n is. I'd swap wid yer any day, I 'clare I would, on'y I dun'no as he'd be so becomin' to me as old dad is; an' like as not I shouldn't be as becomin' to him as you be. So I s'pose, on de whole, we had better each on us keep to our own."

"Yes," said Alice quietly, "I think so too."

"But, Alice, I don't like yer goin' home to de old country; I don't see how I can spare yer. I don't brame yer, nuther; I'd go wid yer if it wuz not for my old pardner here. If ole dad would on'y die now! but he won't—he aint got no proper feelin' for me, dat ole man haint. He wouldn't inconvene hisself—he wouldn't jest *die*—no, not to obleedge de best frien' he haz in de world—and dat's me; no he wouldn't. An' I don't jest like to turn my back on him after keepin' him on so long; but I really tink he grows tougher an' stronger ebery day he libs. An' why shouldn't he, when he eats all he can get, right hand and lef' hand, fit to beat all nater?"

"Oh, Winny, Winny! do let the poor old man have enough to eat."

"Enuff! yes, ob course—but what is enuff? I'd like to know dat; you don't know, an' I'm sure he don't. Why, he'll eat all I can sot afore him, an' den, if anudder chance comes along, he's ready for it—he'll jest turn to, an' eat jest as much more.

Enuff! I 'clare, he neber 'lowed he had it yet, an' I guess he neber will."

Still Winny did grieve deeply for the loss of her friends with a genuine sorrow, for which not all the liberal provision they had made for the support of herself and her father in their declining years could compensate. Not even Alice's last laughing injunction to her to " be sure and let old Drosky have as much to eat as was good for him," could bring to the dark face of the sorrowing old woman one of her broadly good-natured smiles.

CHAPTER XXIII.

THE CONCLUSION.

"Through all its varying scenes our tale has run—
The story's ended, and the play is done;
Let fall the curtain, and put out the light—
Then, 'exeunt omnes'—and to all 'good-night.'"

ND now, having disposed of the more important *dramatis personæ* of our story, but little more remains to bring it to its conclusion.

The terrible delusion of witchcraft, upon which this narrative is founded, had a sudden rise, but it had a still more sudden termination; the monstrous evil had sprung up and swelled, until it burst by the innate force of its own virulence; it was like one of those vile poisonous fungi which spring up in a night, scattering sickness and death around, and disappear forever.

Perhaps the wretched girls who figured so

prominently in its horrors, and whose demoniac performances had so shocked the public mind and dethroned all the calmer powers of reason, had become wearied of their deadly sport; or else, confident in their success hitherto, they had become reckless of consequences.; but it is certain they went too far and struck too high.

They had accused the wife of Philip English, one of the most prominent merchants of Salem, who had escaped from jail, and saved her life by flight; and also the Rev. Samuel Williard, minister of the Old South Church, in Boston; and the mother-in-law of Justice Corwin, an estimable lady residing in Boston (probably because he was too passive at the. trials to suit them); and now, in October, they ventured to accuse Mrs. Hale, the wife of the minister of the First Church in Beverly: her genuine excellence and sweet womanly graces and virtues were widely known; the community, through undoubting faith in her, became convinced of the daring perjury of the accusers, and their power was at an end. "Never was a revolution so sudden and so complete, and the great body of the people were rescued from their delusion."

All the previous trials had been held by a special court, which was now superseded, and a permanent and regular tribunal, the Superior Court of Judicature, was then established. They held their first court in January, 1693, and continued their sessions until May—although no new condemnations appear to have been made by them; and in May, Sir William Phips, the governor, by a general proclamation, discharged all the prisoners.

The number thus set free is said to have been about one hundred and fifty. Twenty had been executed—some had died in prison—a considerable number had broken from jail and made their escape; and it has been estimated that the whole number of persons who had been committed on charge of this imaginary crime amounted to several hundreds.

But even after this legal acquittal, the prisoners were not set at liberty until they had paid all the charges for their board while in prison, and all the court and jailor's fees; by

this cruel refinement of extortion, these helpless beings, who had already had their homes
and possessions despoiled, were reduced in
many instances to utter impoverishment.

In looking back upon this terrible tragedy,
even after the long lapse of years, there seems
to be no way to account for it by any of the
known and recognized laws of the human
mind; the actors in it seem to have been
utterly reckless of consequences to others,
and totally incapable of human feeling.
There is no mention on record of their being
once moved by natural pity for the sufferings they wrought; and in one instance, one
of the girls explained her unfounded charge
as having been " only in *sport*—we must
have *some sport*." And they seem to have
been in a gay, frivolous state of mind, as if
totally unconscious of the death-dealing nature of their accusations; and even after the
delusion had passed by, although some few
of the older and more important persons in-
volved in this fearful loss of life have left a
noble record of their true repentance and re-
morse for the delusion into which they had
suffered themselves to be drawn, the girls

do not give any evidence that they had any realizing sense of the enormity of the sin they had committed. In their subsequent confessions they speak of their conduct by such mild terms as "an error of judgment, a strange delusion of the devil," rather than in a spirit of heartfelt repentance for their terrible guilt, and its widespread and irre-mediable effects.

Even the Reverend Mr. Parris appears himself so entirely devoid of natural human sympathies that he was positively unable to realize their existence in others: "He could not be made to understand why the sorrow-ing family of Rebecca Nurse felt themselves so much aggrieved by her cruel and unjust execution; he told them in plain terms that while they thought her innocent, and he be-lieved her guilty and justly put to death, "it was a mere difference of opinion;" as if he regarded the fact of her life or death as an altogether indifferent matter."

But the history of the Past is the warning of the Future—the beacon that shows where one frail little bark went down has saved many a gallant vessel from a similar fate;

and if the terrible delusion of 1692 has taught our magistrates and rulers caution and temperate judgment—if the sacred fear of taking human life even from the worst of criminals which pervades our jury-boxes, and has sometimes been regarded as almost pusillanimity, has sprung from a remembrance of the terrible era when the judgment of the whole community—legal, ecclesiastical, and secular—swerved aside and was bent like a reed before the breath of passion and superstition, the annals of "Salem Witchcraft" have not been preserved in vain.

VALUABLE AND INTERESTING WORKS

FOR

PUBLIC & PRIVATE LIBRARIES,

PUBLISHED BY HARPER & BROTHERS, NEW YORK.

☞ *For a full List of Books suitable for Libraries, see* HARPER & BROTHERS' TRADE-LIST *and* CATALOGUE, *which may be had gratuitously on application to the Publishers personally, or by letter enclosing Six Cents in Postage Stamps.*

☞ HARPER & BROTHERS *will send any of the following works by mail, postage prepaid, to any part of the United States, on receipt of the price.*

FLAMMARION'S ATMOSPHERE. The Atmosphere. Translated from the French of CAMILLE FLAMMARION. Edited by JAMES GLAISHER, F.R.S., Superintendent of the Magnetical and Meteorological Department of the Royal Observatory at Greenwich. With 10 Chromo-Lithographs and 86 Woodcuts. 8vo, Cloth, $6 00.

HUDSON'S HISTORY OF JOURNALISM. Journalism in the United States, from 1690 to 1872. By FREDERICK HUDSON. Crown 8vo, Cloth, $5 00.

PIKE'S SUB-TROPICAL RAMBLES. Sub-Tropical Rambles in the Land of the Aphanapteryx. By NICOLAS PIKE, U. S. Consul, Port Louis, Mauritius. Profusely Illustrated from the Author's own Sketches; containing also Maps and Valuable Meteorological Charts. Crown 8vo, Cloth, $3 50.

TRISTRAM'S THE LAND OF MOAB. The Result of Travels and Discoveries on the East Side of the Dead Sea and the Jordan. By H. B. TRISTRAM, M.A., LL.D., F.R.S., Master of the Greatham Hospital, and Hon. Canon of Durham. With a Chapter on the Persian Palace of Mashita, by JAS. FERGUSON, F.R.S. With Map and Illustrations. Crown 8vo, Cloth, $2 50.

SANTO DOMINGO, Past and Present; with a Glance at Hayti. By SAMUEL HAZARD. Maps and Illustrations. Crown 8vo, Cloth, $3 50.

LIFE OF ALFRED COOKMAN. The Life of the Rev. Alfred Cookman; with some Account of his Father, the Rev. George Grimston Cookman. By HENRY B. RIDGAWAY, D.D. With an Introduction by Bishop FOSTER, LL.D. Portrait on Steel. 12mo, Cloth, $2 00.

HERVEY'S CHRISTIAN RHETORIC. A System of Christian Rhetoric, for the Use of Preachers and Other Speakers. By GEORGE WINFRED HERVEY, M.A., Author of "Rhetoric of Conversation," &c. 8vo, Cloth, $3 50.

CASTELAR'S OLD ROME AND NEW ITALY. Old Rome and New Italy. By EMILIO CASTELAR. Translated by Mrs. ARTHUR ARNOLD. 12mo, Cloth, $1 75.

THE TREATY OF WASHINGTON: Its Negotiation, Execution, and the Discussions Relating Thereto. By CALEB CUSHING. Crown 8vo, Cloth, $2 00.

PRIME'S I GO A-FISHING. I Go a-Fishing. By W. C. PRIME. Crown 8vo, Cloth, $2 50.

HALLOCK'S FISHING TOURIST. The Fishing Tourist: Angler's Guide and Reference Book. By CHARLES HALLOCK. Illustrations. Crown 8vo, Cloth, $2 00.

SCOTT'S AMERICAN FISHING. Fishing in American Waters. By GENIO C. SCOTT. With 170 Illustrations. Crown 8vo, Cloth, $3 50.

ANNUAL RECORD OF SCIENCE AND INDUSTRY FOR 1872. Edited by Prof. Spencer F. Baird, of the Smithsonian Institution, with the Assistance of Eminent Men of Science. 12mo, over 700 pp., Cloth, $2 00. (Uniform with the *Annual Record of Science and Industry for* 1871. 12mo, Cloth, $2 00.)

COL. FORNEY'S ANECDOTES OF PUBLIC MEN. Anecdotes of Public Men. By John W. Forney. 12mo, Cloth, $2 00.

MISS BEECHER'S HOUSEKEEPER AND HEALTHKEEPER: Containing Five Hundred Recipes for Economical and Healthful Cooking; also, many Directions for securing Health and Happiness. Approved by Physicians of all Classes. Illustrations. 12mo, Cloth, $1 50.

FARM BALLADS. By Will Carleton. Handsomely Illustrated. Square 8vo, Ornamental Cloth, $2 00; Gilt Edges, $2 50.

POETS OF THE NINETEENTH CENTURY. The Poets of the Nineteenth Century. Selected and Edited by the Rev. Robert Aris Willmott. With English and American Additions, arranged by Evert A. Duyckinck, Editor of "Cyclopædia of American Literature." Comprising Selections from the Greatest Authors of the Age. Superbly Illustrated with 141 Engravings from Designs by the most Eminent Artists. In elegant small 4to form, printed on Superfine Tinted Paper, richly bound in extra Cloth, Beveled, Gilt Edges, $5 00; Half Calf, $5 50; Full Turkey Morocco, $9 00.

THE REVISION OF THE ENGLISH VERSION OF THE NEW TESTAMENT. With an Introduction by the Rev. P. Schaff, D.D. 618 pp., Crown 8vo, Cloth, $3 00.

This work embraces in one volume:

  I. ON A FRESH REVISION OF THE ENGLISH NEW TESTAMENT. By J. B. Lightfoot, D.D., Canon of St. Paul's, and Hulsean Professor of Divinity, Cambridge. Second Edition, Revised. 196 pp.

  II. ON THE AUTHORIZED VERSION OF THE NEW TESTAMENT in Connection with some Recent Proposals for its Revision. By Richard Chenevix Trench, D.D., Archbishop of Dublin. 194 pp.

  III. CONSIDERATIONS ON THE REVISION OF THE ENGLISH VERSION OF THE NEW TESTAMENT. By C. J. Ellicott, D.D., Bishop of Gloucester and Bristol. 178 pp.

NORDHOFF'S CALIFORNIA. California: For Health, Pleasure, and Residence. A Book for Travelers and Settlers. Illustrated. 8vo, Paper, $2 00; Cloth, $2 50.

MOTLEY'S DUTCH REPUBLIC. The Rise of the Dutch Republic. By John Lothrop Motley, LL.D., D.C.L. With a Portrait of William of Orange. 3 vols., 8vo, Cloth, $10 50.

MOTLEY'S UNITED NETHERLANDS. History of the United Netherlands: from the Death of William the Silent to the Twelve Years' Truce —1609. With a full View of the English-Dutch Struggle against Spain, and of the Origin and Destruction of the Spanish Armada. By John Lothrop Motley, LL.D., D.C.L. Portraits. 4 vols., 8vo, Cloth, $14 00.

NAPOLEON'S LIFE OF CÆSAR. The History of Julius Cæsar. By His late Imperial Majesty Napoleon III. Two Volumes ready. Library Edition, 8vo, Cloth, $3 50 per vol.

HAYDN'S DICTIONARY OF DATES, relating to all Ages and Nations. For Universal Reference. Edited by Benjamin Vincent, Assistant Secretary and Keeper of the Library of the Royal Institution of Great Britain: and Revised for the Use of American Readers. 8vo, Cloth, $5 00; Sheep, $6 00.

MACGREGOR'S ROB ROY ON THE JORDAN. The Rob Roy on the Jordan, Nile, Red Sea, and Gennesareth, &c. A Canoe Cruise in Palestine and Egypt, and the Waters of Damascus. By J. Macgregor, M.A. With Maps and Illustrations. Crown 8vo, Cloth, $2 50.

WALLACE'S MALAY ARCHIPELAGO. The Malay Archipelago: the Land of the Orang-Utan and the Bird of Paradise. A Narrative of Travel, 1854-1862. With Studies of Man and Nature. By ALFRED RUSSEL WALLACE. With Ten Maps and Fifty-one Elegant Illustrations. Crown 8vo, Cloth, $2 50.

WHYMPER'S ALASKA. Travel and Adventure in the Territory of Alaska, formerly Russian America—now Ceded to the United States—and in various other parts of the North Pacific. By FREDERICK WHYMPER. With Map and Illustrations. Crown 8vo, Cloth, $2 50.

ORTON'S ANDES AND THE AMAZON. The Andes and the Amazon: or, Across the Continent of South America. By JAMES ORTON, M.A., Professor of Natural History in Vassar College, Poughkeepsie, N. Y., and Corresponding Member of the Academy of Natural Sciences, Philadelphia. With a New Map of Equatorial America and numerous Illustrations. Crown 8vo, Cloth, $2 00.

WINCHELL'S SKETCHES OF CREATION. Sketches of Creation: a Popular View of some of the Grand Conclusions of the Sciences in reference to the History of Matter and of Life. Together with a Statement of the Intimations of Science respecting the Primordial Condition and the Ultimate Destiny of the Earth and the Solar System. By ALEXANDER WINCHELL, LL.D., Chancellor of the Syracuse University. With Illustrations. 12mo, Cloth, $2 00.

WHITE'S MASSACRE OF ST. BARTHOLOMEW. The Massacre of St. Bartholomew: Preceded by a History of the Religious Wars in the Reign of Charles IX. By HENRY WHITE, M.A. With Illustrations. 8vo, Cloth, $1 75.

LOSSING'S FIELD-BOOK OF THE REVOLUTION. Pictorial Field-Book of the Revolution; or, Illustrations, by Pen and Pencil, of the History, Biography, Scenery, Relics, and Traditions of the War for Independence. By BENSON J. LOSSING. 2 vols., 8vo, Cloth, $14 00; Sheep, $15 00; Half Calf, $18 00; Full Turkey Morocco, $22 00.

LOSSING'S FIELD-BOOK OF THE WAR OF 1812. Pictorial Field-Book of the War of 1812; or, Illustrations, by Pen and Pencil, of the History, Biography, Scenery, Relics, and Traditions of the Last War for American Independence. By BENSON J. LOSSING. With several hundred Engravings on Wood, by Lossing and Barritt, chiefly from Original Sketches by the Author. 1088 pages, 8vo, Cloth, $7 00; Sheep, $8 50; Half Calf, $10 00.

ALFORD'S GREEK TESTAMENT. The Greek Testament: with a critically revised Text; a Digest of Various Readings; Marginal References to Verbal and Idiomatic Usage; Prolegomena; and a Critical and Exegetical Commentary. For the Use of Theological Students and Ministers. By HENRY ALFORD, D.D., Dean of Canterbury. Vol. I., containing the Four Gospels. 944 pages, 8vo, Cloth, $6 00; Sheep, $6 50.

ABBOTT'S FREDERICK THE GREAT. The History of Frederick the Second, called Frederick the Great. By JOHN S. C. ABBOTT. Elegantly Illustrated. 8vo, Cloth, $5 00.

ABBOTT'S HISTORY OF THE FRENCH REVOLUTION. The French Revolution of 1789, as viewed in the Light of Republican Institutions. By JOHN S. C. ABBOTT. With 100 Engravings. 8vo, Cloth, $5 00.

ABBOTT'S NAPOLEON BONAPARTE. The History of Napoleon Bonaparte. By JOHN S. C. ABBOTT. With Maps, Woodcuts, and Portraits on Steel. 2 vols., 8vo, Cloth, $10 00.

ABBOTT'S NAPOLEON AT ST. HELENA; or, Interesting Anecdotes and Remarkable Conversations of the Emperor during the Five and a Half Years of his Captivity. Collected from the Memorials of Las Casas, O'Meara, Montholon, Antommarchi, and others. By JOHN S. C. ABBOTT. With Illustrations. 8vo, Cloth, $5 00.

ADDISON'S COMPLETE WORKS. The Works of Joseph Addison, embracing the whole of the "Spectator." Complete in 3 vols., 8vo, Cloth, $6 00.

ALCOCK'S JAPAN. The Capital of the Tycoon: a Narrative of a Three Years' Residence in Japan. By Sir RUTHERFORD ALCOCK, K.C.B., Her Majesty's Envoy Extraordinary and Minister Plenipotentiary in Japan. With Maps and Engravings. 2 vols., 12mo, Cloth, $3 50.

ALISON'S HISTORY OF EUROPE. FIRST SERIES: From the Commencement of the French Revolution, in 1789, to the Restoration of the Bourbons, in 1815. [In addition to the Notes on Chapter LXXVI., which correct the errors of the original work concerning the United States, a copious Analytical Index has been appended to this American Edition.] SECOND SERIES: From the Fall of Napoleon, in 1815, to the Accession of Louis Napoleon, in 1852. 8 vols., 8vo, Cloth, $16 00.

BARTH'S NORTH AND CENTRAL AFRICA. Travels and Discoveries in North and Central Africa: being a Journal of an Expedition undertaken under the Auspices of H.B.M.'s Government, in the Years 1849–1855. By HENRY BARTH, Ph.D., D.C.L. Illustrated. 3 vols., 8vo, Cloth, $12 00.

HENRY WARD BEECHER'S SERMONS. Sermons by HENRY WARD BEECHER, Plymouth Church, Brooklyn. Selected from Published and Unpublished Discourses, and Revised by their Author. With Steel Portrait. Complete in 2 vols., 8vo, Cloth, $5 00.

LYMAN BEECHER'S AUTOBIOGRAPHY, &c. Autobiography, Correspondence, &c., of Lyman Beecher, D.D. Edited by his Son, CHARLES BEECHER. With Three Steel Portraits, and Engravings on Wood. In 2 vols., 12mo, Cloth, $5 00.

BOSWELL'S JOHNSON. The Life of Samuel Johnson, LL.D. Including a Journey to the Hebrides. By JAMES BOSWELL, Esq. A New Edition, with numerous Additions and Notes. By JOHN WILSON CROKER, LL.D., F.R.S. Portrait of Boswell. 2 vols., 8vo, Cloth, $4 00.

DRAPER'S CIVIL WAR. History of the American Civil War. By JOHN W. DRAPER, M.D., LL.D., Professor of Chemistry and Physiology in the University of New York. In Three Vols. 8vo, Cloth, $3 50 per vol.

DRAPER'S INTELLECTUAL DEVELOPMENT OF EUROPE. A History of the Intellectual Development of Europe. By JOHN W. DRAPER, M.D., LL.D., Professor of Chemistry and Physiology in the University of New York. 8vo, Cloth, $5 00.

DRAPER'S AMERICAN CIVIL POLICY. Thoughts on the Future Civil Policy of America. By JOHN W. DRAPER, M.D., LL.D., Professor of Chemistry and Physiology in the University of New York. Crown 8vo, Cloth, $2 50.

DU CHAILLU'S AFRICA. Explorations and Adventures in Equatorial Africa, with Accounts of the Manners and Customs of the People, and of the Chase of the Gorilla, the Crocodile, Leopard, Elephant, Hippopotamus, and other Animals. By PAUL B. DU CHAILLU. Numerous Illustrations. 8vo, Cloth, $5 00.

DU CHAILLU'S ASHANGO LAND. A Journey to Ashango Land: and Further Penetration into Equatorial Africa. By PAUL B. DU CHAILLU. New Edition. Handsomely Illustrated. 8vo, Cloth, $5 00.

BELLOWS'S OLD WORLD. The Old World in its New Face: Impressions of Europe in 1867–1868. By HENRY W. BELLOWS. 2 vols., 12mo, Cloth, $3 50.

BRODHEAD'S HISTORY OF NEW YORK. History of the State of New York. By JOHN ROMEYN BRODHEAD. 1609–1691. 2 vols. 8vo, Cloth, $3 00 per vol.

BROUGHAM'S AUTOBIOGRAPHY. Life and Times of HENRY, LORD BROUGHAM. Written by Himself. In Three Volumes. 12mo, Cloth, $2 00 per vol.

BULWER'S PROSE WORKS. Miscellaneous Prose Works of Edward Bulwer, Lord Lytton. 2 vols., 12mo, Cloth, $3 50.

BULWER'S HORACE. The Odes and Epodes of Horace. A Metrical Translation into English. With Introduction and Commentaries. By Lord Lytton. With Latin Text from the Editions of Orelli, Macleane, and Yonge. 12mo, Cloth, $1 75.

BULWER'S KING ARTHUR, A Poem. By Lord Lytton. New Edition. 12mo, Cloth, $1 75.

BURNS'S LIFE AND WORKS. The Life and Works of Robert Burns. Edited by Robert Chambers. 4 vols., 12mo, Cloth, $6 00.

REINDEER, DOGS, AND SNOW-SHOES. A Journal of Siberian Travel and Explorations made in the Years 1865-'67. By Richard J. Bush, late of the Russo-American Telegraph Expedition. Illustrated. Crown 8vo, Cloth, $3 00.

CARLYLE'S FREDERICK THE GREAT. History of Friedrich II., called Frederick the Great. By Thomas Carlyle. Portraits, Maps, Plans, &c. 6 vols., 12mo, Cloth, $12 00.

CARLYLE'S FRENCH REVOLUTION. History of the French Revolution. 2 vols., 12mo, Cloth, $3 50.

CARLYLE'S OLIVER CROMWELL. Letters and Speeches of Oliver Cromwell. With Elucidations and Connecting Narrative. 2 vols., 12mo, Cloth, $3 50.

CHALMERS'S POSTHUMOUS WORKS. The Posthumous Works of Dr. Chalmers. Edited by his Son-in-Law, Rev. William Hanna, LL.D. Complete in 9 vols., 12mo, Cloth, $13 50.

COLERIDGE'S COMPLETE WORKS. The Complete Works of Samuel Taylor Coleridge. With an Introductory Essay upon his Philosophical and Theological Opinions. Edited by Professor Shedd. Complete in Seven Vols. With a Portrait. Small 8vo, Cloth, $10 50.

DOOLITTLE'S CHINA. Social Life of the Chinese: with some Account of their Religious, Governmental, Educational, and Business Customs and Opinions. With special but not exclusive Reference to Fuhchau. By Rev. Justus Doolittle, Fourteen Years Member of the Fuhchau Mission of the American Board. Illustrated with more that 150 characteristic Engravings on Wood. 2 vols., 12mo, Cloth, $5 00.

GIBBON'S ROME. History of the Decline and Fall of the Roman Empire. By Edward Gibbon. With Notes by Rev. H. H. Milman and M. Guizot. A new cheap Edition. To which is added a complete Index of the whole Work, and a Portrait of the Author. 6 vols., 12mo, Cloth, $9 00.

HAZEN'S SCHOOL AND ARMY IN GERMANY AND FRANCE. The School and the Army in Germany and France, with a Diary of Siege Life at Versailles. By Brevet Major-General W. B. Hazen, U.S.A., Colonel Sixth Infantry. Crown 8vo, Cloth, $2 50.

HARPER'S NEW CLASSICAL LIBRARY. Literal Translations.

The following Vols. are now ready. 12mo, Cloth, $1 50 each.

Cæsar.—Virgil.—Sallust.—Horace.—Cicero's Orations.—Cicero's Offices, &c.—Cicero on Oratory and Orators.—Tacitus (2 vols.).—Terence.—Sophocles.—Juvenal.—Xenophon.—Homer's Iliad.—Homer's Odyssey. — Herodotus. — Demosthenes. — Thucydides. — Æschylus.—Euripides (2 vols.).—Livy (2 vols.).

DAVIS'S CARTHAGE. Carthage and her Remains: being an Account of the Excavations and Researches on the Site of the Phœnician Metropolis in Africa and other adjacent Places. Conducted under the Auspices of Her Majesty's Government. By Dr. Davis, F.R.G.S. Profusely Illustrated with Maps, Woodcuts, Chromo-Lithographs, &c. 8vo, Cloth, $4 00.

EDGEWORTH'S (Miss) NOVELS. With Engravings. 10 vols., 12mo, Cloth, $15 00.

GROTE'S HISTORY OF GREECE. 12 vols., 12mo, Cloth, $18 00.

HELPS'S SPANISH CONQUEST. The Spanish Conquest in America, and its Relation to the History of Slavery and to the Government of Colonies. By ARTHUR HELPS. 4 vols., 12mo, Cloth, $6 00.

HALE'S (MRS.) WOMAN'S RECORD. Woman's Record; or, Biographical Sketches of all Distinguished Women, from the Creation to the Present Time. Arranged in Four Eras, with Selections from Female Writers of Each Era. By Mrs. SARAH JOSEPHA HALE. Illustrated with more than 200 Portraits. 8vo, Cloth, $5 00.

HALL'S ARCTIC RESEARCHES. Arctic Researches and Life among the Esquimaux: being the Narrative of an Expedition in Search of Sir John Franklin, in the Years 1860, 1861, and 1862. By CHARLES FRANCIS HALL. With Maps and 100 Illustrations. The Illustrations are from the Original Drawings by Charles Parsons, Henry L. Stephens, Solomon Eytinge, W. S. L. Jewett, and Granville Perkins, after Sketches by Captain Hall. 8vo, Cloth, $5 00.

HALLAM'S CONSTITUTIONAL HISTORY OF ENGLAND, from the Accession of Henry VII. to the Death of George II. 8vo, Cloth, $2 00.

HALLAM'S LITERATURE. Introduction to the Literature of Europe during the Fifteenth, Sixteenth, and Seventeenth Centuries. By HENRY HALLAM. 2 vols., 8vo, Cloth, $4 00.

HALLAM'S MIDDLE AGES. State of Europe during the Middle Ages. By HENRY HALLAM. 8vo, Cloth, $2 00.

HILDRETH'S HISTORY OF THE UNITED STATES. FIRST SERIES: From the First Settlement of the Country to the Adoption of the Federal Constitution. SECOND SERIES: From the Adoption of the Federal Constitution to the End of the Sixteenth Congress. 6 vols., 8vo, Cloth, $18 00.

HUME'S HISTORY OF ENGLAND. History of England, from the Invasion of Julius Cæsar to the Abdication of James II., 1688. By DAVID HUME. A new Edition, with the Author's last Corrections and Improvements. To which is Prefixed a short Account of his Life, written by Himself. With a Portrait of the Author. 6 vols., 12mo, Cloth, $9 00.

JAY'S WORKS. Complete Works of Rev. William Jay: comprising his Sermons, Family Discourses, Morning and Evening Exercises for every Day in the Year, Family Prayers, &c. Author's enlarged Edition, revised. 3 vols., 8vo, Cloth, $6 00.

JEFFERSON'S DOMESTIC LIFE. The Domestic Life of Thomas Jefferson: compiled from Family Letters and Reminiscences, by his Great-Granddaughter, SARAH N. RANDOLPH. With Illustrations. Crown 8vo, Illuminated Cloth, Beveled Edges, $2 50.

JOHNSON'S COMPLETE WORKS. The Works of Samuel Johnson, LL.D. With an Essay on his Life and Genius, by ARTHUR MURPHY, Esq. Portrait of Johnson. 2 vols., 8vo, Cloth, $4 00.

KINGLAKE'S CRIMEAN WAR. The Invasion of the Crimea, and an Account of its Progress down to the Death of Lord Raglan. By ALEXANDER WILLIAM KINGLAKE. With Maps and Plans. Two Vols. ready. . 12mo, Cloth, $2 00 per vol.

KINGSLEY'S WEST INDIES. At Last: A Christmas in the West Indies. By CHARLES KINGSLEY. Illustrated. 12mo, Cloth, $1 50.

KRUMMACHER'S DAVID, KING OF ISRAEL. David, the King of Israel: a Portrait drawn from Bible History and the Book of Psalms. By FREDERICK WILLIAM KRUMMACHER, D.D., Author of "Elijah the Tishbite," &c. Translated under the express Sanction of the Author by the Rev. M. G. EASTON, M.A. With a Letter from Dr. Krummacher to his American Readers, and a Portrait. 12mo, Cloth, $1 75.

LAMB'S COMPLETE WORKS. The Works of Charles Lamb. Comprising his Letters, Poems, Essays of Elia, Essays upon Shakspeare, Hogarth, &c., and a Sketch of his Life, with the Final Memorials, by T. NOON TALFOURD. Portrait. 2 vols., 12mo, Cloth, $3 00.

LIVINGSTONE'S SOUTH AFRICA. Missionary Travels and Researches in South Africa; including a Sketch of Sixteen Years' Residence in the Interior of Africa, and a Journey from the Cape of Good Hope to Loando on the West Coast; thence across the Continent, down the River Zambesi, to the Eastern Ocean. By David Livingstone, LL.D., D.C.L. With Portrait, Maps by Arrowsmith, and numerous Illustrations. 8vo, Cloth, $4 50.

LIVINGSTONES' ZAMBESI. Narrative of an Expedition to the Zambesi and its Tributaries, and of the Discovery of the Lakes Shirwa and Nyassa. 1858–1864. By David and Charles Livingstone. With Map and Illustrations. 8vo, Cloth, $5 00.

M'CLINTOCK & STRONG'S CYCLOPÆDIA. Cyclopædia of Biblical, Theological, and Ecclesiastical Literature. Prepared by the Rev. John M'Clintock, D.D., and James Strong, S.T.D. 5 vols. now ready. Royal 8vo, Price per vol., Cloth, $5 00; Sheep, $6 00; Half Morocco, $8 00.

MARCY'S ARMY LIFE ON THE BORDER. Thirty Years of Army Life on the Border. Comprising descriptions of the Indian Nomads of the Plains; Explorations of New Territory; a Trip across the Rocky Mountains in the Winter; Descriptions of the Habits of Different Animals found in the West, and the Methods of Hunting them; with Incidents in the Life of Different Frontier Men, &c., &c. By Brevet Brigadier-General R. B. Marcy, U.S.A., Author of "The Prairie Traveller." With numerous Illustrations. 8vo, Cloth, Beveled Edges, $3 00.

MACAULAY'S HISTORY OF ENGLAND. The History of England from the Accession of James II. By Thomas Babington Macaulay. With an Original Portrait of the Author. 5 vols., 8vo, Cloth, $10 00; 12mo, Cloth, $7 50.

MOSHEIM'S ECCLESIASTICAL HISTORY, Ancient and Modern; in which the Rise, Progress, and Variation of Church Power are considered in their Connection with the State of Learning and Philosophy, and the Political History of Europe during that Period. Translated, with Notes, &c., by A. Maclaine, D.D. A new Edition, continued to 1826, by C. Coote, LL.D. 2 vols., 8vo, Cloth, $4 00.

THE DESERT OF THE EXODUS. Journeys on Foot in the Wilderness of the Forty Years' Wanderings; undertaken in connection with the Ordnance Survey of Sinai and the Palestine Exploration Fund. By E. H. Palmer, M.A., Lord Almoner's Professor of Arabic, and Fellow of St. John's College, Cambridge. With Maps and numerous Illustrations from Photographs and Drawings taken on the spot by the Sinai Survey Expedition and C. F. Tyrwhitt Drake. Crown 8vo, Cloth, $3 00.

OLIPHANT'S CHINA AND JAPAN. Narrative of the Earl of Elgin's Mission to China and Japan, in the Years 1857, '58, '59. By Laurence Oliphant, Private Secretary to Lord Elgin. Illustrations. 8vo, Cloth, $3 50.

OLIPHANT'S (Mrs.) LIFE OF EDWARD IRVING. The Life of Edward Irving, Minister of the National Scotch Church, London. Illustrated by his Journals and Correspondence. By Mrs. Oliphant. Portrait. 8vo, Cloth, $3 50.

RAWLINSON'S MANUAL OF ANCIENT HISTORY. A Manual of Ancient History, from the Earliest Times to the Fall of the Western Empire. Comprising the History of Chaldæa, Assyria, Media, Babylonia, Lydia, Phœnicia, Syria, Judæa, Egypt, Carthage, Persia, Greece, Macedonia, Parthia, and Rome. By George Rawlinson, M.A., Camden Professor of Ancient History in the University of Oxford. 12mo, Cloth, $2 50.

RECLUS'S THE EARTH. The Earth: A Descriptive History of the Phenomena and Life of the Globe. By Élisée Reclus. Translated by the late B. B. Woodward, and Edited by Henry Woodward. With 234 Maps and Illustrations and 23 Page Maps printed in Colors. 8vo, Cloth, $5 00.

RECLUS'S OCEAN. The Ocean, Atmosphere, and Life. Being the Second Series of a Descriptive History of the Life of the Globe. By Élisée Reclus. Profusely Illustrated with 250 Maps or Figures, and 27 Maps printed in Colors. 8vo, Cloth, $6 00.

SHAKSPEARE. The Dramatic Works of William Shakspeare, with the Corrections and Illustrations of Dr. JOHNSON, G. STEVENS, and others. Revised by ISAAC REED. Engravings. 6 vols, Royal 12mo, Cloth, $9 00. 2 vols., 8vo, Cloth, $4 00.

SMILES'S LIFE OF THE STEPHENSONS. The Life of George Stephenson, and of his Son, Robert Stephenson; comprising, also, a History of the Invention and Introduction of the Railway Locomotive. By SAMUEL SMILES, Author of "Self-Help," &c. With Steel Portraits and numerous Illustrations. 8vo, Cloth, $3 00.

SMILES'S HISTORY OF THE HUGUENOTS. The Huguenots: their Settlements, Churches, and Industries in England and Ireland. By SAMUEL SMILES. With an Appendix relating to the Huguenots in America. Crown 8vo, Cloth, $1 75.

SPEKE'S AFRICA. Journal of the Discovery of the Source of the Nile. By Captain JOHN HANNING SPEKE, Captain H.M. Indian Army, Fellow and Gold Medalist of the Royal Geographical Society, Hon. Corresponding Member and Gold Medalist of the French Geographical Society, &c. With Maps and Portraits and numerous Illustrations, chiefly from Drawings by Captain GRANT. 8vo, Cloth, uniform with Livingstone, Barth, Burton, &c., $4 00.

STRICKLAND'S (MISS) QUEENS OF SCOTLAND. Lives of the Queens of Scotland and English Princesses connected with the Regal Succession of Great Britain. Py AGNES STRICKLAND. 8 vols., 12mo, Cloth, $12 00.

THE STUDENT'S SERIES.
France. Engravings. 12mo, Cloth, $2 00.
Gibbon. Engravings. 12mo, Cloth, $2 00.
Greece. Engravings. 12mo, Cloth, $2 00.
Hume. Engravings. 12mo, Cloth, $2 00.
Rome. By Liddell. Engravings. 12mo, Cloth, $2 00.
Old Testament History. Engravings. 12mo, Cloth, $2 00.
New Testament History. Engravings, 12mo, Cloth, $2 00.
Strickland's Queens of England. Abridged. Eng's. 12mo, Cloth, $2 00.
Ancient History of the East. 12mo, Cloth, $2 00.
Hallam's Middle Ages. 12mo, Cloth, $2 00.
Hallam's Constitutional History of England. 12mo, Cloth, $2 00.
Lyell's Elements of Geology. 12mo, Cloth, $2 00.

TENNYSON'S COMPLETE POEMS. The Complete Poems of Alfred Tennyson, Poet Laureate. With numerous Illustrations by Eminent Artists, and Three Characteristic Portraits. 8vo, Paper, 75 cents; Cloth, $1 25.

THOMSON'S LAND AND THE BOOK. The Land and the Book; or, Biblical Illustrations drawn from the Manners and Customs, the Scenes and the Scenery of the Holy Land. By W. M. THOMSON, D.D., Twenty-five Years a Missionary of the A.B.C.F.M. in Syria and Palestine. With two elaborate Maps of Palestine, an accurate Plan of Jerusalem, and several hundred Engravings, representing the Scenery, Topography, and Productions of the Holy Land, and the Costumes, Manners, and Habits of the People. 2 large 12mo vols., Cloth, $5 00.

TYERMAN'S WESLEY. The Life and Times of the Rev. John Wesley, M.A., Founder of the Methodists. By the Rev. LUKE TYERMAN. Portraits. 3 vols., Crown 8vo, Cloth, $7 50.

TYERMAN'S OXFORD METHODISTS. The Oxford Methodists: Memoirs of the Rev. Messrs. Clayton, Ingham, Gambold, Hervey, and Broughton, with Biographical Notices of others. By the Rev. L. TYERMAN. With Portraits. Crown 8vo, Cloth, $2 50.

VÁMBÉRY'S CENTRAL ASIA. Travels in Central Asia. Being the Account of a Journey from Teheren across the Turkoman Desert, on the Eastern Shore of the Caspian, to Khiva, Bokhara, and Samarcand, performed in the Year 1863. By ARMINIUS VÁMBÉRY, Member of the Hungarian Academy of Pesth, by whom he was sent on this Scientific Mission. With Map and Woodcuts. 8vo, Cloth, $4 50.

WOOD'S HOMES WITHOUT HANDS. Homes Without Hands: being a Description of the Habitations of Animals, classed according to their Principle of Construction. By J. G. WOOD, M.A., F.L.S. With about 140 Illustrations. 8vo, Cloth, Beveled Edges, $4 50.